Dora

Praise for Malorie Bla

Noughts & Crosses
'A book which will linger in the mind long after it has been read'
Observer

Knife Edge
'A powerful story of race and prejudice' *Sunday Times*

Checkmate
'Another emotional hard-hitter . . .
bluntly told and ingeniously constructed' *Sunday Times*

Double Cross
'Blackman "gets" people . . . she "gets" humanity as a whole, too.
Most of all, she writes a stonking good story' *Guardian*

Boys Don't Cry
'Shows her writing at its best, creating characters and a story which,
once read, will not easily go away' *Independent*

Pig-Heart Boy
'A powerful story about friendship, loyalty and family' *Guardian*

Hacker
'Refreshingly new . . . Malorie Blackman writes
with such winsome vitality' *Telegraph*

A.N.T.I.D.O.T.E.
'Strong characterisation and pacy dialogue make this a real winner'
Independent

Thief!
'. . . impossible to put down' *Sunday Telegraph*

Dangerous Reality
'A whodunnit, a cyber-thriller and a family drama: readers of nine or
over won't be able to resist the suspense' *Sunday Times*

www.**malorieblackman**.co.uk

**By Malorie Blackman and published
by Doubleday/Corgi Books:**

malorie
blackman

CORGI BOOKS

HACKER
A CORGI BOOK 978 0 552 55164 9

First published in Great Britain by Doubleday,
an imprint of Random House Children's Publishers UK
A Random House Group Company

Doubleday edition published 1992
Corgi edition published 1993
Corgi edition reissued 2004

This edition published 2011

3 5 7 9 10 8 6 4

Set in Bembo

Corgi Books are published by Random House Children's Publishers UK,
61–63 Uxbridge Road, London W5 5SA

www.**randomhouse**.co.uk
www.**randomhousechildrens**.co.uk
www.**totallyrandombooks**.co.uk

Addresses for companies within The Random House Group Limited can be found at:
www.randomhouse.co.uk/offices.htm

THE RANDOM HOUSE GROUP Limited Reg. No. 954009

A CIP catalogue record for this book is available from the British Library.

Printed and bound by CPI Group (UK) Ltd, Croydon, CR0 4YY

For Neil and Lizzy,
with love

Chapter One

The Start of the Bad Times

Maths exams! Ugh!

It was a toast-warm Friday afternoon in May. The kind of afternoon when all you wanted to do was sunbathe and fan yourself. But end-of-year exams had come around again, and all us Boroughvale Year 9s had a maths exam ahead of us. I was near the front of the queue to get into the exam room, and my brother Gib and his friend Chaucy were only a few behind me. I was pretending to talk to my friend Maggie, but really I was earwigging on Gib and Chaucy's conversation.

'I should be lying down in the garden with a ginormous chocolate milkshake and a whole packet of chocolate digestives all to myself,' Gib said.

Typical of you – pig! I thought.

'I know what you mean.' Chaucy sighed. 'I think I'd rather be at the dentist having all my teeth filled than having to spend the afternoon trying to answer unanswerable maths questions.'

'Well, I'd rather be in a leaky canoe in a crocodile-infested river,' Gib said.

Chaucy laughed. 'I'd rather be naked at the North Pole.'

'Amateur!' Gib scoffed. 'I'd rather be kissed by Vicky . . . on second thoughts, no I wouldn't!'

I spun around. 'If I kissed you, brat-face, my lips would probably drop off!'

Were real brothers as rotten as Gib always was to me? I wondered. He was only my brother because his mum and dad had adopted me when I was a baby. Then they were unlucky enough to have him. It would have been so lovely to have been an only child!

'I wasn't talking to you, Vicky. Don't stick this . . .' Gib tapped his nose with his finger, 'where it isn't wanted.'

I glared at him and Chaucy. Chaucy was grinning at me, enjoying Gib's put-down. Chaucy – or Alexander Chaucer as it said on the school register – wasn't as bad as Gib, but he was sure heading that way. He was at least half a head taller than Gib but he followed my scabby brother around everywhere – like a sheep or a puppy dog. Chaucy was pretty average, except for his hair. It seemed to alternate between a speckled chocolate brown and a dusty black, depending on how the light hit it. It made him look as if his hair was permanently full of dandruff.

What I didn't like about Chaucy was that he was

always laughing at me. I stuck my tongue out at both of them and turned back to my friend, Maggie. I wished I was the sort of person who could think of really funny, razor-sharp retorts on the spur of the moment, but I never could. I always came up with something really clever and funny to say about two days after the event. Gib's good at thinking on his feet, though. He has an answer for everything.

'Never mind them,' Maggie said loftily. 'They're so juvenile.'

That was her current favourite word. Maggie read the dictionary the way I read Harry Potter books. Each week she'd pick out a new word and then she'd bore us all silly by using it in practically every other sentence.

'Did you revise, Vicky?' she asked.

'Nah, not really,' I shrugged. 'Did you?'

Maggie shook her head. 'No. I tried to but . . . no.'

I smiled at Maggie. I reckoned she'd probably been up most nights in the past week revising hard, just like I'd done.

Why do we never own up to revising? I wondered. But I guess I knew why really. No one wanted to fail their exams, but at the same time who wanted to be called an egg-head or a boffin? And worse still, what if you *did* say you'd revised hard and then you failed . . .? Shame!

Just then, the assembly hall doors opened. Mrs Bracken stood in the doorway, peering at us through her glasses which were thicker than double-glazing. They were even thicker than my glasses – and that's saying something!

'Less noise, please,' she shouted at the top of her lungs. 'You may all come in now.'

As soon as I walked into the hall, I wrinkled up my nose at the cheesy smell of feet and old shoes. There'd obviously been a PE lesson in the hall that morning. I grabbed a desk right in the middle of the hall and sat down. The sounds of chairs being dragged across the wooden floor, the clatter of pens and pencils in polythene bags and pencil-cases, worried whispers and subdued coughs filled the air. At last, even those noises died away as everyone settled down in their seats. I had to shuffle for a good minute before I got as comfortable as I was going to get. The chair seats were rock hard.

'Right then, who needs a school calculator?' Mrs Bracken called out. A forest of arms appeared and waved in the air. Mrs Bracken and Mr Peterson walked around the hall, each carrying a large cardboard box from which they distributed the calculators. I didn't need one. I had my own calculator which Dad and Mum had bought me for Christmas. After the calculators were given out, Mrs Bracken walked up onto the stage and slowly scanned the hall with her beady eyes. Mr Peterson was still walking up and down and Mrs Canon, my geography teacher, sat in a chair at the side of the hall, reading through the maths paper.

Mrs Bracken turned her attention to the huge clock on the wall, so we all did. Its slow *tchlock, tchlock* echoed in the hall as every second was marked up to two o'clock.

'You may begin,' she said at last.

Instantly, the hall was alive with the rustle of papers. This term, the maths exam covered trigonometry and polygons. I flicked through the exam. Boring but not *too* bad . . .

I looked around to see what Gib was doing. I caught sight of him almost immediately. He was staring down at the first page of the five-page exam. Then he turned to the next page, then the next and the next. As I watched, he flicked through the exam paper again, hoping no doubt that with a second reading the questions would change. They didn't! He slumped in his chair and rested his shiny, perspiring forehead on his hand. He knew and I knew that he was in deep, *deep* trouble! I couldn't resist a bit of a smirk! Really mean, I know, but he deserved it for being such a pig!

I took a quick glance around the hall. Shivvy, the egg-head, was stuffing three peppermints into her mouth at once. She'd probably come out of the hall at the end boasting about how easy the exam had been. She's a real swot and a half, that one.

There was Tristan in his new navy-blue jacket which he refused to take off for anyone. I was sure he even slept in it. Then, as I watched, Tristan pushed up his jacket sleeve to read what he'd written on his shirt cuff. I couldn't believe it. If I was going to fail, at least I was going to do it under my own steam. I directed the filthiest look I could at him then turned away in disgust, hoping he would see me.

But everyone was at it!

My friend Maggie had her nose buried inside her pencil-case and I could see writing on the inside of the case even from where I was sitting. I was shocked. I could understand Tristan cheating – he couldn't write his name without looking on his shirt sleeve first – but Maggie?

I felt a sudden strange prickling all over my skin. I looked up and there was Crackly Bracken, watching me. Hastily I looked down at my paper and picked up my pen. I didn't want her to think that *I* was cheating. I studied the first question. My trouble was that I could learn the basic rules but I had some trouble applying them if I didn't think for ages about it first.

After a good five minutes thinking how I should do question one, I picked up my calculator. That's when I had my mega-brilliant idea. I looked from the exam paper to my calculator and back again. I'm OK at maths, but computing is *my* subject – if that's not boasting. (I think it probably is!)

And my calculator was programmable. It looked like an ordinary calculator, except the display screen was a little bigger, and I'd written programs on it lots of times before. So why not just write a program to work out interior and exterior angles and lengths and areas and all the other stuff? I had all the necessary functions on my calculator. I could program it without even having to think about it – much!

Feeling very pleased with myself, I took a piece of paper and started to work out how I should write my program. After that, I typed it into my calculator. All in all it only took about twenty minutes. Then I whizzed through the maths questions in about two minutes flat. Just to make sure that I hadn't got my program wrong, I worked out the first, tenth and last questions by hand on a spare piece of paper. My answers were the same as the calculator's so I knew I had got them right.

I wanted to jump up and down on my chair I was so chuffed. I put my pen down and leaned back with my arms folded. I glanced up at the hall clock. It was only half-past two. I'd finished my test in *half an hour*. I couldn't help it. I started grinning and grinning.

'Victoria Gibson, get on with the test.' Mrs Bracken's voice boomed out, making me jump.

I looked up at her and smiled. 'I've finished, miss,' I said.

Instantly, I could feel every eye in the hall upon me. It felt really good! My grin broadened. I could almost feel my head growing bigger too!

'*What* did you say?' Mrs Bracken asked.

'I've finished the exam, miss,' I repeated.

7

Mrs Bracken stood up abruptly, the legs of her chair scraping against the wooden floor of the stage. As she marched down the steps, butterflies appeared from nowhere and started to flutter in my stomach. She made straight for me and snatched up my paper. Her eyes narrowed as she scrutinized each and every page.

For the first time I thought about exactly what I'd done. This was supposed to be a maths exam not a computing exam. Maybe I shouldn't have used my calculator to get the answers . . . ? Slowly I slid my calculator over the piece of paper I'd used to work out the design of my program. Then I casually covered the calculator with my hand.

'I . . . I told you I'd finished,' I said.

I only said that so that Mrs Bracken would look at me and not at what my hand was doing. Mrs Bracken straightened up to scowl at me and the butterflies in my stomach turned into stampeding rhinos.

'So it was you, was it . . . ? Pick up your things, Victoria, and follow me.' Mrs Bracken had a face like thunder.

'What's the matter?' I whispered.

'Do as you're told,' she hissed at me.

I scrambled to pick up all the items on my desk. Something told me I was in mega-trouble. I stood up.

'Is there anyone else who claims to have finished?' Mrs Bracken asked.

Her piercing gaze darted over everyone else in the

assembly hall. I looked around. As soon as I caught anyone's eye, they looked away or down at their desk. I saw Gib. He had sunk into his chair, trying to look as small as possible as Mrs Bracken and I looked at him. My head, my entire body, now felt about the size of a pea. And you could have cooked several eggs on my face, no bother at all.

'Victoria, follow me,' Mrs Bracken ordered.

Clutching my papers and sweets and my calculator to me, desperate not to drop them, I followed Mrs Bracken out of the assembly hall. I still didn't understand what was wrong. Maybe she knew about my calculator being programmable . . .

Mrs Bracken shut the hall door carefully behind me. 'And where did you get the answers from?' she asked me stonily. 'As if we didn't know.'

I stared up at her, thinking I must have misheard.

'P-pardon?' I stammered.

'You heard me. Don't pretend you don't know what I'm talking about. You and I both know how every one of your answers happens to be correct.'

I didn't even feel good when I heard her say that. I knew I was in seriously serious trouble.

'Miss, I don't understand . . .' I began.

'Victoria, there is no way you could have finished this test in . . .' Mrs Bracken glanced down at her watch, 'in thirty-three minutes, unless you already knew the answers.'

9

'But I didn't . . . How could . . . ?'

'Don't compound your crime by lying, child.'

'But I'm not . . .'

'So you just read the questions and automatically knew the answers?' Mrs Bracken's eyebrows were so low they touched her eyelashes.

'No . . . n-not exactly . . .'

'You didn't show how you worked out any of your answers. There are no jottings on your answer paper, no workings, nothing. Or are you telling me that you worked out the answers to all my questions in your head?'

'N-not exactly,' I said. 'I u-used my calculator . . .'

'Don't be facetious, child.'

'I really did.'

Mrs Bracken didn't let me finish. 'Not another word. You're a cheat, Victoria Gibson,' she said furiously.

That word made me jump. I wasn't a cheat. I'd never cheated at anything in my life.

'Mrs Bracken, if you'd just let me explain . . .' I began again. I rummaged through all the stuff in my arms to dig out my calculator. 'I didn't cheat. I—'

'You don't have to explain, Victoria. I know exactly how you did it. I knew I'd catch the culprit. But I must say, I'm surprised it's you. I thought you knew better.'

Culprit? What culprit? What was she talking about?

Mrs Bracken folded her hands across her ample

10

chest. 'We are going to see the headmistress,' she said with satisfaction.

At that, my heart tried to burst out of my chest. My face was burning, boiling hot, and I felt absolutely sick.

'We're going to see Miss Hiff . . . ?' The words came out in a dismayed squeak.

'Yes. Miss Hiff,' Mrs Bracken said with relish.

'But I didn't cheat, miss . . .'

'Of course you did,' Mrs Bracken said icily. 'When it comes to maths, Victoria, you are no Einstein, and not even Einstein could have finished my test in the short amount of time it took you – unless he previously had the answers, of course.'

Previously had the answers . . . ? I felt like I'd started watching telly halfway through a really confusing film. How could I have previously had the answers? I programmed my calculator to work out the answers. My eyes were really stinging now and there was a whole football stuck in my throat, choking me.

'I'm surprised at you, Victoria, I really am. But I'll tell you something. When I've finished with you,' Mrs Bracken bent over suddenly so that her face was only centimetres away from mine and her breath felt horribly warm and moist on my face, 'when I've finished with you, my girl, you'll wish you'd never done it. Now follow me.'

Chapter Two

The Letter

Mrs Bracken made me wait outside Miss Hiff's office for ages before she finally opened the door to let me in. Whiffy Hiffy's usually not too bad — in the past she'd always smiled at me whenever we passed each other in the corridor — but I took one look at her face and I didn't feel any better.

What have you been saying about me? I thought, and scowled at Mrs Bracken.

Whatever it was, it hadn't been very pleasant. That much was obvious from Miss Hiff's expression. My heart was dancing like a Mexican jumping bean as I stood in front of the headmistress. Her office was small and square, with grey filing cabinets against one wall and a huge wooden table just in front of the window. Miss Hiff sat behind the table, her arms folded and resting on it as she leaned forward. She had dark brown eyes and black hair with streaks of grey all through it. We all called her Whiffy Hiffy because she wore a really strong perfume that smelt of flowers and made you want to sneeze.

'I have just one question to ask you, Vicky, and I want you to tell me the truth,' Miss Hiff began. 'I know how good at programming you are. Did you work out these answers yourself, or did they come courtesy of your considerable computer skills?'

I tried to think of something to say that wouldn't get me into worse trouble. OK, so I'd used my own calculator instead of one of the school's prehistoric ones. But no one had ever said I couldn't. The thought popped into my head that no one had ever said I *could* either, but I made it pop out again.

'I'm waiting, Vicky,' Miss Hiff said.

'I . . . er . . .'

'Yes or no?' Miss Hiff asked.

'Yes . . . I did, but . . .'

Miss Hiff leaned back in her chair. 'I see. I'm disappointed in you, Victoria. Deeply disappointed. So you admit that you cheated?'

'I never said that,' I replied hotly. 'I . . . I didn't exactly see it as cheating.'

'Then how did you see it – exactly?' Miss Hiff asked sternly.

'Well, no one ever said I couldn't do it,' I muttered, which was a big mistake because I should have kept that little thought to myself.

'Victoria! I can't believe you said that. You know a lot better than that,' Miss Hiff said sharply.

'But, Miss Hiff, I—'

'No buts, Victoria. I can't imagine what you were thinking of. This was a maths exam, not a test of computational deviousness. Not that I would have approved of your methods in the latter case. Did you really think we wouldn't catch you?' Miss Hiff leaned even further forward over her desk. Her brown eyes glinted like marbles.

'No . . . yes . . . I mean . . .' I didn't know what I meant. 'I guess I didn't really think about it . . . really . . . I thought I was being clever . . .'

'Clever! Do you realize that at the very least I'm going to have to suspend you?' Miss Hiff asked.

I felt like I'd been hit in the stomach. I stared at her so hard I'm surprised my eyes didn't pop out of my head and plop on to the carpet.

'Suspend . . . ? You're joking,' I whispered.

'Do I look like I'm joking?' Miss Hiff said stonily. 'This is very serious, Victoria, very serious indeed. You cheated to get the answers to your maths exam and not only that but you were disgracefully rude with it. I would never have thought it of you. I have your mother's phone number at work, so I'll give her a call and ask her to come and see me . . .'

'NO! No, you can't. You can't phone Mum.' I didn't mean to shout but I could feel myself beginning to panic. Mum and Dad . . . What on earth would they say about all this? And how was I rude? How was it rude to use a calculator?

'And why not?' Miss Hiff asked.

I took a quick look at Mrs Bracken who stood beside me, shaking her head down at me. I could just hear 'the youth of today' or one of her other soppy phrases rattling around in her head. I turned back to the head-mistress. I couldn't believe it. I was going to be suspended for using my calculator. Was this fair or what?

'M-mum is . . . she isn't well,' I said reluctantly.

'Oh? What's wrong with her?' asked Miss Hiff.

I swallowed hard. This was horrible. Now I'd have to talk about private family stuff.

'Mum . . . Mum's six months pregnant. And she's not very well. She has high blood pressure and she's only just been let out of hospital. Her doctor said she's got to take it easy and she mustn't get upset.'

Every part of Miss Hiff's face seemed to be frowning. Her lips were turned down, her eyes were turned down, even the many lines on her forehead bent down at the ends.

'Very well then. I shall phone your father,' Miss Hiff said.

'Oh, couldn't you call him on Monday?' I pleaded. 'Friday is his busiest day at the bank.'

'I can't help that,' Miss Hiff said firmly. 'Mrs Bracken, would you get Mr Gibson's work number from the school secretary.'

If she ran any faster, she'd take off! I thought as Mrs Bracken fairly sprinted from the room.

'Vicky, now that we're alone is there anything you'd like to tell me before I phone your father?' asked Miss Hiff.

Like what? I thought.

'No.' I shook my head.

'Is everything OK at home?' Miss Hiff asked gently.

My face felt like it was on fire. I knew what she was getting at. Did my parents quarrel or did my mum throw saucepans at my dad or me or something equally ridiculous. I got on fine with Mum and Dad. In fact, Dad and I spent a lot of time together. He was the one who got me interested in computing in the first place and he was teaching me all about the computer system at his bank. And if Gib and I had the occasional quarrel, so what? All brothers and sisters argue sometimes.

'Vicky?' Miss Hiff prompted.

'Everything's fine, miss,' I said. I was so embarrassed I just wanted to crawl under Miss Hiff's table.

'Then why did you do it? I'm at a loss to under-stand . . .'

'Here we are, Miss Hiff.' Mrs Bracken walked back into the office, closing the door behind her. 'This is Victoria's card.'

A small index card was handed to the headmistress. She picked up the phone and dialled. I tried to read what was on it but it was too far away and upside down at that.

'Ah, good morning,' Miss Hiff said almost

16

immediately, 'I'd like to speak to Mr David Gibson, please.'

There was a pause and then the headmistress repeated her request.

'Yes, that's right – Mr Gibson . . . Oh, I see . . . Oh, I see . . . no, I'm the headmistress of Boroughvale School . . . I wanted to talk to him about his daughter . . . Oh, I see . . . All right then. Thank you for your help.' Miss Hiff put the phone down. She was frowning even more now.

'Your father's not there and he won't be back today,' Miss Hiff explained.

It was my turn to frown now. Dad was always at the bank on Fridays. If he wasn't there, then where was he?

'It seems as if I'm destined not to speak to either of your parents today, but I want to see your father early next week without fail. Wait outside whilst I write a letter to him and your mother.'

Mrs Bracken ushered me outside. I racked my brains for something to say that would sort all this out, but there was nothing in my head and nothing in my mouth. The story of my life! All I could think about was what Mum and Dad would say. I'd never been in trouble at school before. That was usually Gib's department. Mum and Dad were always saying to him, 'Why can't you be more like your sister?'

As I stood outside Miss Hiff's office, I realized I'd never hear Mum and Dad ask that particular question again.

Suspended.

Even Gib had never been suspended. He'd never even come close and he was always getting into trouble. And now I'd outdone him – in one fell swoop. But that wasn't the worst of it.

What were Mum and Dad going to say?

'Vicky! Vicky, wait for me!'

Stupidly, I turned my head to see Gib legging it after me, his jacket off his shoulders and his school bag waving about all over the place as he ran. I carried on walking even faster. Gib was the last person I wanted to speak to.

'Didn't you hear me calling you?' Gib puffed angrily once he'd caught up with me.

'What do you want?' I snapped.

'I want to make sure you're all right,' Gib said.

I stopped walking and looked him straight in the eye at that.

'Do I look like I'm stupid? Don't answer that!' I said quickly as Gib opened his mouth to reply. 'You just want to know what Whiffy Hiffy said to me – nosy git-bag!'

Gib started to smile. 'Well, you can't blame me. So what *did* Miss Hiff say?' The smile on his face was getting bigger and bigger.

'None of your business,' I replied. I started walking again.

'Oh, go on. I won't tell anyone,' Gib cajoled.

'Don't be so bloomin' nosy,' I said, glaring at him.

'Don't be like that,' Gib said, 'I'm only asking. Did she expel you?'

'NO, SHE DID NOT!' I exploded. 'At least . . . at least, not yet. If you must know, she asked me if I'd used my calculator to answer all the questions in the maths exam correctly. When I said yes, she went on and on about how cheating was beneath me and how I ought to be ashamed of myself. Then she made me sit outside her office for the rest of the afternoon. I didn't cheat . . . at least, I didn't realize I was cheating. I didn't *mean* to cheat, unlike some people I saw whom I could mention. But Mum and Dad aren't going to care about that. They're both going to go through the ceiling!'

I slowed down. Walking so fast was making my legs ache. Gib fell into line next to me. We very rarely walked home together so it felt slightly strange.

'Your calculator? I don't understand. How can you cheat using a grotty school calculator?' Gib said.

'I . . . I used the programmable calculator Mum and Dad bought me for Christmas to answer the questions,' I admitted. 'I still don't see what all the fuss is about. Just because I didn't use one of the stupid, diddly school calculators.'

'So how did you do it?' Gib asked.

I could see he was impressed, even though he tried his best not to show it. I shrugged. 'I wrote a program

19

to do it for me. Then all I had to do was input the number of sides a shape had and any of the angles as given on the exam paper, or input any of the other details and get back the proper angles and areas and whatnot. It was a doddle.'

'So Mrs Bracken told Hiffy that you used your calculator?' Gib asked.

'And she probably took great pleasure in doing it as well,' I sighed.

We walked on for a while in silence. Then Gib said, 'You didn't help your own case much by leaning back in your chair, grinning up at the assembly hall clock. I saw you. Very subtle – I don't think!'

'I wouldn't have done it if I'd known they were going to get all nuclear about it,' I said with disgust. 'If I was Mrs Bracken I would have been impressed with my ingenuity . . .'

'Instead of which, you get accused of cheating.' Gib's lips twitched.

'I'm glad one of us thinks this is funny,' I said angrily. 'I should have known I wouldn't get much sympathy from you.' I marched away from him, sorry I'd said a word.

'Hang on, Vicky. I'm sorry. So what *did* happen? Did you get detention next week or what?' Gib asked, jogging after me.

Slowly, I shook my head. 'I wouldn't mind if it was just detention. I wouldn't even mind detention for the

20

rest of the term. But . . . but Miss Hiff wants to see Dad on Monday and she's talking about suspending me.'

'*Suspending you?*' Gib repeated, astounded. 'Wow! Mum and Dad aren't going to like that.'

'Why don't you do an A level in the bloomin' obvious,' I hissed. 'You'd get an A star.'

'Don't take it out on me,' Gib snapped back. 'I didn't tell you to cheat.'

'I *didn't* cheat!' I shouted. 'I didn't see it as cheating for a single second.'

'Then you'd better hope that Dad and Mum agree with you and see it your way and not Miss Hiff's.'

Pushing my hand further into my jacket pocket, I fingered the envelope Miss Hiff had given me for Mum and Dad.

'They won't see my side of things,' I sighed. 'Not after they see this.'

I took out the now grubby and crumpled envelope and showed it to Gib. Miss Hiff had signed her name across the back flap of the envelope and stuck it down with at least three pieces of Sellotape. The front of the envelope had Mum and Dad's names as well as our address typed on it.

'Do you know what it says?' Gib asked, turning it over in his hands.

'I haven't a clue. But I can guess.'

Gib nodded. 'So what are you going to do?'

'What d'you think I should do?' I asked.

Gib looked straight at me. 'Open it.'

'I can't do that,' I said aghast. 'I'm in enough trouble as it is. I can't just . . .'

Gib raised his hands. 'It's all right. I knew you wouldn't do it. You don't have the guts.'

'Guts have nothing to do with it,' I argued. 'I've just as much guts as you or anyone.'

'Then prove it. Open it.'

'OK, genius. And just how do I stick it back down afterwards? I'll never get Miss Hiff's signature to line up again.'

'Simple,' Gib said so glibly that I wanted to chuck a bucket of ice-cold water over him. 'You type out another envelope and put the letter in that. Mum and Dad will never know that Miss Hiff's signature was on the back of the original.'

'There speaks an expert,' I said sourly.

Now, usually I would have told Gib where to go after making a suggestion like that. I've got a lot more common sense than he has, but he's only a boy so what do you expect? But at that moment all I could think about was getting suspended from school and how Dad would be disappointed and how Mum would get upset, especially when she wasn't supposed to. So I thought, if only I knew what the letter said then I could prepare them – and me – for the worst.

Gib handed the letter back to me and I held it gingerly, staring down at it. It was as if the envelope was burning my fingers and it wouldn't stop burning my fingers until I knew what Miss Hiff had written about me.

'I . . . I don't know . . .' I said, doubtfully.

'Go on. I won't tell. I promise,' Gib urged.

I took a deep breath. Before I could change my mind, I tore off the left-hand piece of sticky tape and stuck my finger under the flap. I pulled it up. I told myself I couldn't get into any worse trouble, but deep down I knew I could. It still didn't stop me.

'What does it say? What does it say?' Gib said eagerly. He pulled my arm over to him.

I pulled back indignantly. 'I think I should read it first, don't you?'

'Then read it to me,' Gib said impatiently.

I didn't really want to, but I didn't see how it could make much difference now. Besides, Gib might tell Mum and Dad what I'd done if I didn't tell him what was in the letter. He wasn't usually a snitch but he could be a real pig when he didn't get his own way.

Dear Mr and Mrs Gibson,
   I deeply . . .

I didn't get any further. Gib's head was in my way where he'd moved in for a closer look.

'You make a better door than a window,' I said sarcastically. 'Move your fat head!'

He glowered at me but he did move. I carried on reading.

I deeply regret to inform you that today your daughter, Victoria, was caught cheating in her end-of-term maths exam. Mrs Bracken, your daughter's maths teacher, prepared the exam on her personal computer. Yesterday morning, when Mrs Bracken returned to her PC, she found an unseemly message – signed by 'Hacker Supreme' – which had been left at the top of the file containing the maths exam answers.

Today, when confronted, your daughter admitted to using her programming skills to get into this file and read the answers. I'm sure you'll agree with me that this is a very serious matter indeed and it could well lead to Victoria's expulsion. I am at a loss to understand what made her do it as Victoria has been, to date, an exemplary pupil. Please could you phone me or my secretary, Mrs Goater, to arrange a mutually convenient meeting at the beginning of next week.

Best wishes,
Miss Julia Hiff

'Wow! Double wow!' Gib breathed. 'I thought you said you used your programmable calculator.'

'I *did*,' I squeaked.

I re-read the letter again and a third time. If it wasn't for the fact that it was addressed to Mr and Mrs Gibson,

I would have been sure that Miss Hiff had given me the wrong letter.

'Well, when you were talking about your calculator, they were obviously talking about Mrs Bracken's PC,' Gib said, re-reading the letter himself.

'What am I going to do?' I said. 'I can't show this to Mum and Dad.'

'So you're not the person who left that message for Mrs Bracken on her PC?' Gib asked.

'Of course not!' That was the closest I'd ever got to wanting to hit him. 'I wouldn't do something like that. I didn't know anything about it until a minute ago.'

'If you didn't do it, I wonder who did?' Gib mused.

'That's not the burning issue at the moment,' I snapped. 'What am I going to do?'

'No problem. Just tell Mum and Dad that you mis-understood what Miss Hiff was talking about and vice versa,' Gib said.

'Suppose they don't believe me?'

'Of course they'll believe you,' Gib snorted. 'Don't they always believe everything you say?'

Something in the way he said that made me frown as I looked at him, but I let it pass.

'What about Miss Hiff? She can still suspend me. And it'll be for something I haven't done,' I said.

'Just tell her the same thing you tell Mum and Dad. They'll back you up.'

He made it sound so easy. I wished I had his

confidence. Shaking my head, I read the letter again but the words didn't change. I stuffed the rotten thing back in my pocket and wondered what I should do.

'What else could possibly go wrong?' I said fiercely.

When we got home I found out.

'Mum, we're home,' Gib called out once we were inside our house. I knew something was wrong, even before Mum appeared. Usually, as soon as I set foot over the doormat, all kinds of delicious dinner smells hit me: sausages and beans and fried bananas (my favourite) or pizza or grilled fish (yuk!) – but always something. Today there was nothing at all. Mum walked into the hall from the living room, her hand resting on her bulging stomach. Her eyes looked strange. Kind of starey and hard. And Mum usually smiled at us when we got home from school, but now her lips were a thin, pursed line across her face. Even her normally neat and tidy hair looked as if she'd been running her fingers through it over and over again.

'Mum, what's the matter?' I asked.

'Come in here, you two,' Mum sniffed. 'I've got something to tell you.'

'It's not the baby, is it?' Gib said. 'Mum, you should be sitting down. You should be resting.'

'This is more important,' Mum said dismissively, running her fingers absent-mindedly through her hair as she led the way into the living room. Gib and I sat down on the sofa while Mum paced up and down in front of us. She kept opening and closing her mouth, but nothing was coming out. It was as if she just couldn't find the words.

'What is it, Mum?' I asked anxiously.

I was so worried. I couldn't remember when I'd ever seen Mum so upset, so close to tears. She sat down carefully in the armchair opposite us. She kept twisting her fingers over and over in her lap.

'I've always been honest with you two and I'm not going to change that now,' Mum said at last. 'I've got some bad news.'

'You're all right, aren't you?' Gib asked.

'I'm . . . OK. But I want you two to prepare yourselves. It . . . it's your father.'

'What about him?' Gib said before I could. 'He hasn't had an accident, has he?'

'No, dear.' Mum took a deep breath. 'He's been arrested.'

Chapter Three

Some Home Truths

'Arrested?'

'You must be joking!'

'For what?'

I stared at Mum, utterly shocked. I think I was more shocked than if she had said that Dad had been knocked over. When she'd said she had bad news, I thought, Dad's hurt. He's in hospital. But not for a single second would I have guessed he'd been arrested.

'Your dad was arrested earlier this morning,' Mum said. She could hardly get the words out. She sounded as if she was choking on something. 'Some money turned up in his bank account at the bank and he can't explain how it got there.'

'Money? How much money turned up?' Gib asked.

Mum didn't answer straight away. Her hands twisted faster and faster in her lap. I looked at Gib and he looked at me. There had to be some kind of mistake. Some horrible, ghastly mistake.

Arrested . . . It was a word you heard on the telly and

in films, not something that happened to your dad in real life. I looked at Mum. I couldn't take my eyes off her. The silence in the room was deafening.

'How much money, Mum?' Gib asked again.

Mum swallowed hard. 'The bank says that your dad took . . . took over a million pounds . . .'

'One mill . . .' I coughed. I couldn't get the word out.

'The million with six zeroes in it?' Gib squeaked.

'Just over.' Mum nodded.

'They must be crazy. If Dad had that kind of money we'd all be living on our own island somewhere,' Gib said scornfully.

'This isn't funny, Gib.' I rounded on him.

'Do you see me laughing?' Gib snapped back.

Mum was about to tell us both off when the door-bell rang.

'Who on earth is that?' Mum frowned.

She stood up and went to open the door. I couldn't think. Nothing would come into my head. I sat absolutely still, trying to force myself to concentrate on what Mum had just said.

Arrested . . . This had to be a joke . . . or a mistake. A horrible mistake. Dad arrested . . . Where was he now? How was he feeling? I turned to look at Dad's PC which sat, rather self-consciously, on its own table in the corner opposite the telly.

One million pounds. All that money in Dad's

account . . . How had it got there? Dad hadn't put it there, I knew he hadn't.

'Aunt Beth!' Gib sprang up off the sofa.

I turned my head to see Mum follow Aunt Beth and her husband Sebastian into the room. Mum sat down in the armchair, while Aunt Beth sat down in the space Gib had left for her on the sofa. Sebastian stood leaning against the door frame.

'Hello, Aunt Beth,' I said. 'I didn't know you were coming round tonight.' I had to force myself to speak normally. I wasn't sure if Aunt Beth knew what had happened.

Aunt Beth wasn't really our aunt but that's what we'd always called her. She and Dad both worked at Universal Bank, although they worked in separate sections of the computing department. They'd known each other for years. I think Aunt Beth was actually matron-of-honour at Mum and Dad's wedding. So she'd never believe Dad was guilty. She'd be on our side.

Aunt Beth was tall, quite a lot taller than Mum. She wore glasses with bright red frames and her blonde hair was pulled back into its usual ponytail. I'd never seen her hair in any other style. And she was wearing her usual tiny, gold-stud earrings and her necklace with a 'B' hanging from it that she had bought for herself when out shopping with Mum once. I looked past her to Sebastian.

I liked Sebastian. He was Aunt Beth's second

husband. He didn't really say much, but he smiled at me a lot. Sebastian was a manager in one of the big West End department stores – I've forgotten which one.

'Hello, Gib, Vicky.' Aunt Beth smiled. 'Do you mind if I just have a quick word with your mum?'

From the forced smile on her face and the anxious look she gave Mum, I guessed that she knew all about Dad and the business at the bank.

'It's all right, Beth. I've already told them what's happened,' Mum said wearily.

'Is there anything I can do for you, Laura?' Aunt Beth asked Mum.

'No, I don't think so,' Mum sighed. 'I just wish I knew what this was all about. David phoned me from the police station but all he said was that one million pounds went missing from the bank and it was found in his bank account.'

'I'm afraid I don't know much more than that,' Aunt Beth apologized. 'Usually banks like to try and keep this sort of thing quiet, but the sum of money was so large and David is an employee rather than an anonymous hacker from outside, so the General Manager felt she had to call in the police.'

'Why would the bank want to keep it quiet?' Gib asked curiously. 'Surely they've got more chance of getting their money back if they make it public.'

31

''Cause they don't want all the people who keep their money at the bank to think that it isn't safe, of course,' I answered.

'I didn't ask you.' Gib glared at me.

'You're absolutely right, Vicky,' Aunt Beth replied. 'It's silly but there it is.'

'What do you think will happen, Beth?' Mum asked her.

Aunt Beth shrugged. 'I don't know. Nothing like this has ever happened at Universal Bank before. But I think the bank will definitely press charges. They'll want to deter anyone else from trying it. So I guess David will have to appear at a magistrates' court tomorrow and what happens then depends on the magistrate who gets the case. But I'm sure David will be fine. We all know he didn't do it.'

I looked up at Sebastian, watching as he brushed his hair off his forehead. He caught me looking at him and smiled. I smiled back. Somehow, it was better with Aunt Beth and Sebastian here. I could see that Mum was glad they'd come round.

'Will Dad be coming home tonight though?' I asked, my smile fading.

Mum shook her head. 'I don't know,' she sighed. 'Sebastian, Beth, did you drive here? Do you think you could give me a lift to the police station? I want to be with David.'

'Of course we'll drive you there.' Sebastian smiled at

Mum. 'We'll stay with you and drive you back as well if you like.'

'We'll see,' Mum replied. 'I might be there for quite a while.'

An uncomfortable silence fell over us. I forced myself to break it.

'Aunt Beth, when exactly did the money go missing?' I asked.

'Last night, or rather in the early hours of this morning during the batch-job run,' Aunt Beth replied.

'What's the batch-job run?' Gib asked.

'If you transfer money into, or take money out of your bank account, depending on the transaction the new details don't always show up immediately,' Aunt Beth explained. 'All the details that aren't updated straight away are stored in a file on the bank's computers, but the file doesn't get used until the bank's batch job reads that file each night. Then the results of each overnight transaction are held in the transaction log file.'

'Is the batch job just a computer program, then?' Gib asked.

'Since when have you been interested in computer programming? You hate the subject.' I scowled at him.

He was just doing it to impress Aunt Beth. He only went near Dad's PC to play games. Dad and I were the only ones who used it for programming and analytical stuff. ICT at school was my brother's worst subject. Gib glared at me.

33

'Gib, the batch job is really a special set of programs that are scheduled to run each night,' Aunt Beth said quickly, before Gib and I could launch into a full-scale quarrel.

I was barely listening. Something else had popped into my mind.

'Aunt Beth, Dad said that everyone who works at Universal Bank has to have their bank account there,' I began. 'Is that true?'

'Of course. It's one of the bank's rules when you start working for them,' Aunt Beth said.

'Then anyone at the bank who knew what they were doing could have put that money into Dad's bank account,' I said, thinking out loud.

'Really, Vicky,' Mum sighed. 'Who would do such a thing? More to the point, *why* would they do such a thing? No, it's just a misunderstanding, that's all. I'm sure it'll get sorted out.'

I didn't answer. Mum was just trying to reassure Gib and me but somehow – maybe because of the way the day had gone so far – somehow, I didn't think this would be sorted out quite so easily.

'Don't worry, Laura, I'll do everything I can to get this resolved,' Aunt Beth said.

'Thanks, Beth.' Mum smiled. The first real smile I'd seen from her all evening. 'Right then, Gib and Vicky. I don't know when I'll be back, so don't wait up. And don't forget your homework. Don't leave it till Sunday evening the way you two usually do.'

And with that, Mum, Aunt Beth and Sebastian left the room. I still couldn't take it in about Dad being arrested. I felt so helpless. There had to be something I could do, but what? If only . . .

'You rotten cow!' Gib turned on me the moment he heard the front door shut.

I frowned at him. 'What did you call me that for?'

'Thank you very much for showing me up in front of Aunt Beth!' Gib said furiously.

'Oh, that,' I snorted. 'You know as well as I do that you couldn't care less about the batch job and how it works.'

Gib froze with rage. He just stood there scowling at me which made him look even more drippy than usual.

'At least Aunt Beth likes me,' Gib hissed.

'She likes me too,' I said, surprised.

'No she doesn't. No one likes you,' Gib said.

I stopped smiling at that. I stood up. 'Stop talking rubbish,' I said coldly.

'It's not rubbish. No one likes you. You're not wanted. Even your own parents drowned to get away from you.'

Every drop of blood in me froze. I stared at Gib.

'That's a n-nasty, mean thing to s-say . . .'

'It's true though.' Gib's eyes narrowed as he spoke. 'At least Mum and Dad are my real mum and dad. They'll never be yours, no matter what you do or how hard you

35

try to suck up to them. And you'll never be my sister – thank God. You don't belong. I wish you'd go away. I wish you'd disappear . . .'

Gib only stopped talking because he ran out of breath. I stared at him. I had to fight not to blink. My eyes were stinging and my throat was hurting. I tried swallowing hard, but I couldn't stop tears from rolling down my cheeks.

'Vicky . . . I . . .'

'Y-you don't have to say any more,' I interrupted. 'I get the picture.'

Gib opened his mouth to speak again, but I didn't want to hear another word. I ran out of the living room and up to my bedroom. Slamming the door behind me, I flung myself on the bed. I cried and cried until I had a pounding headache and a pain in my chest and I felt terrible. Gib had never said anything like that before. So that's what he'd been thinking all this time.

That thought made me cry even more. I stood up and stumbled over to my dressing-table. Opening the top drawer, I threw my socks aside. I'd been crying so much I was gulping now and I couldn't stop.

There it was, at the bottom of the drawer. The only photograph I had of my real parents. I took it out and looked at it. I walked slowly over to the bed and hugged it to me. Fresh tears rolled down my cheeks. If I didn't stop crying I'd be sick, but I just couldn't stop.

I mean, I'd always felt that I never *quite* belonged –

like a round wooden block in a larger square hole. But me feeling it and Gib saying it were two different things.

I thought about how Mum and Dad and Gib and me would all walk down the street and I'd pretend they were my real family – that I really belonged to them. No one could tell for certain that I didn't. OK, so Dad was black and Mum was white and Gib's colour was lighter than mine, but so what? That didn't prove anything. Mum and Dad *might* have been my real parents.

I admit that sometimes I couldn't help wondering if the way I felt about them would have been different if they were my real parents. When I bought them Christmas and birthday presents, I sometimes wondered if a real daughter would buy them the things that I bought. On my birthday, I would always wonder what my real mum and dad would have bought me. And then I'd tell myself not to be so silly. I didn't think about it all the time, but it was always there at the back of my mind.

I didn't belong – not really.

I didn't belong anywhere.

And Gib was right. I wasn't wanted.

Mum and Dad certainly wouldn't want me now. Not when things were going so badly. I would be in the way. An extra burden. What if Dad went to prison? I could hardly bear the thought. How would Mum cope with a new baby and Gib and me, all by herself? I cried even more at that. I'd never, ever felt so miserable. It was the worst day of my entire life.

37

I curled up in a ball and cried myself to sleep, wondering if Dad was all right and wishing myself a million, zillion miles away.

'Victoria . . . Victoria, dear, wake up.'

It was Mum. I sat up immediately. Mum didn't usually call me Victoria. She stood by the bed, her shoulders slumped, her lips turned down. Her head kept drooping and she'd straighten her neck and raise her head, but it was almost as if her head was too heavy for her neck and shoulders. I'd never seen her look so unhappy. I looked past her . . . but Dad wasn't there. Gib was. And he was looking everywhere except at me.

'Victoria, are you all right?' Mum asked.

'I'm fine,' I lied, running my hand over my face. Mum frowned but said nothing.

'Mum, where's Dad?' I asked.

'Gib, don't lurk behind me. Come inside so I can tell you both together,' Mum said.

Reluctantly, Gib came into my room. Mum sat next to me on the bed. Gib sat next to her.

'Your dad is . . .'

I watched Mum trying to get the words out.

'Your dad is being held at the police station tonight. He'll appear before a magistrate tomorrow morning. Hopefully, he'll be released on bail so he'll be home tomorrow evening.'

'But what happens if he's not released on bail?' I couldn't help asking.

'Let's cross that bridge if and when we get to it,' Mum said firmly. 'Now then, you two – bed!'

Her lips smiled as she spoke, but her eyes didn't. For once Gib and I didn't argue. I cleaned my teeth and waited until I could hear no one on the landing before dashing back to my room. I didn't want to see Mum and I certainly didn't want to see Gib.

Before today I would never have believed it possible to feel so miserable. And my head was killing me.

Where was Dad? Locked up in a police cell some-where – all by himself. I switched off my light and got into bed, sitting up. Was Dad asleep now? Or was he doing the same as me, staring into the darkness? I lay down on my side. Fresh tears ran across the bridge of my nose and down to the pillow. I didn't think I'd sleep for a second, but once I closed my eyes, I was out.

When I awoke, my room was pitch black. I felt snug and warm and sad. Then I remembered why. I lay still and listened but the house was totally silent. The kind of deep silence you only get when it's really late. I turned over to lie on my back and pulled the duvet up around my neck. I still had my headache and my nose was bunged up from all that crying. I stared into the inky darkness of my room and wondered again how Dad was. I was sure that, if they'd only let him, he could find out who had put that money into his bank account and why. Dad was good at that sort of thing. That's why he was the Computer Auditing Manager at the bank. He always said that programming was like solving a good detective story. You had to put the pieces together so that they fitted like a jigsaw, and if you had bugs or mistakes in your program then you had to hunt them down – just like a detective. That's why I liked programming and computing so much. Because I liked puzzles. That's where Dad and I were so alike.

If only I could write a program to get me out of the trouble I was in at school! Or better still, write a program to find out who'd taken all that money from Dad's bank. Next to this business at Dad's bank, my school problems seemed trivial. How about an all-purpose program to solve both of our problems? The idea made me smile, but my smile didn't last long.

Yeah! I thought sadly. Give Dad a couple of days and he could solve this puzzle – no problem.

Only Dad wasn't here.

But I was . . .

I sat up in bed at that thought. And the more I thought about it, the more I kicked myself for not having thought of it sooner. *I* could find out who put that money in Dad's account. Why not? Dad's PC was downstairs and I knew how to set it up so that I could dial into Universal Bank's computer. I even knew the passwords for Dad's two accounts – although Dad didn't know I knew – so logging on would be no problem.

'Yeah, why not?' I said to myself.

For the first time in what seemed like ages I actually felt better. Dad was always telling me that there was no way to do anything on the computer at Universal Bank without leaving some trace of it somewhere in the system. All I had to do was find that trace and back-track. I would go through all the necessary files to see what I could find. And I wasn't going to leave it until the morning either.

'There's no time like the present,' I told myself.

I switched on my bedside lamp, then immediately switched it off again. Mum was such a light sleeper that she could wake up at the sound of a feather being dropped on the landing carpet. I had to make sure I made no noise. I felt around in the darkness for my slippers and shook them out – to get rid of any stray spiders – before putting them on my feet. And as it was Saturday, Mum and Gib might sleep in a bit later too.

I stood up slowly and crept across the room. My eyes were accustomed to the darkness now but I didn't want to take any chances. Every step was cautious. It took me a good two minutes to turn the door handle because I had to be so careful to make sure it wouldn't make a noise. Then I crept along the landing. Mum's door was shut, as was Gib's. I stared at Gib's door for a few seconds before moving on. No doubt he was really pleased with himself for making me cry.

Well, you'll never make me cry again, I promised myself. Never. I crept down the stairs, making sure I didn't step in the middle of any of them where they might creak. That took me ages, too. But it didn't matter.

I was going to prove that Dad was innocent.

Chapter Four

The Break-in

It wasn't until I had closed the living-room door carefully behind me that I dared to relax slightly. I switched on the light. The sudden brightness dazzled me and for a split second I panicked, sure the light would wake up everyone in the house even though the door was shut.

As I booted up the PC and checked the Broadband connection, I wondered anxiously how Mum was coping. So much for not getting upset. I'd have to do all I could to make sure she was all right, and if Gib chose to call that crawling then that was his problem, not mine.

It took longer to make sure I had the settings right than anything else. If I didn't have the right settings, then I'd never get connected to the computer at Universal Bank. I checked to make sure that the speaker volume was turned right down. Chewing nervously on my bottom lip, I clicked on the GIBSON LOGON icon which automatically went via the Internet to attach to the bank's computer network. Dad had created the

43

connect program to save typing in the same instructions over and over again every time he wanted to log on. The program meant that all he had to do was enter the bank's network code and his password and the program did the rest.

I'd watched Dad go through the whole thing often enough to memorize the bank's network code and password so that was no problem, but as I entered it, I still anxiously watched the screen. I didn't dare breathe. Something was bound to go wrong. I was doing it, so it just had to!

Another worry I had was that a computer operator on night shift at the bank might discover I was logged on to the bank's system. Still, I couldn't let that stop me. As far as the bank was concerned, the million pounds was found in Dad's account and that was all there was to it. I knew Dad didn't do it because he would never do such a thing. I remembered that once he'd found a twenty-pound note in the street and he'd headed straight for the police station.

'That could be some poor pensioner's money,' Dad told me.

Half of me admired him for being so honest, the other half thought Dad was a right mug!

'Most people who found money in the street would keep it,' I said.

'But I'm not most people.' Dad smiled.

And now he was locked up in a police cell

somewhere. I tried to force that thought out of my head before the stinging in my eyes got any worse.

At last the PC was connected to the network at Universal Bank. On the screen it said:

UNIVERSAL BANK NETWORK SYSTEMS

Enter username: GIBSON

Enter password:

then appeared. I'd seen Dad type in the passwords to both of his accounts so that was easy, but I hesitated before typing it in. My stomach was dipping and diving. I couldn't help feeling that I was doing something, if not wrong, then not quite right either. Dad didn't know that I knew his passwords, and he'd hit the roof if he found out. And more than that, I'd never logged on to the bank's computer by myself before. Dad usually did all this, only letting me do the basic, trivial stuff like typing and printing out files.

But now I was alone. And Dad needed my help. Swallowing down my nervousness, I typed in Dad's password – VICRIC2.

ACCESS DENIED. PLEASE CONTACT SYSTEM MANAGER

I frowned at the screen. I'd seen Dad use this account plenty of times and I'd never seen that message before. Thinking that I must have typed in the password incorrectly, I tried it again, carefully pressing each key. V–I–C–R–I–C–2.

The same message appeared. I sat back in my chair, wondering what the matter was. I'd spelt the password right – I was sure I had. I leaned forward to try for a third time, just in case. The living-room door suddenly opened. I almost jumped out of my skin with fright. I turned my head, my finger ready on the PC's ON/OFF button.

It was Gib.

We watched each other. Neither of us said a word. I couldn't think of anything to say. I didn't want to speak to him – not after what had happened earlier. Gib's hair was sticking up in tufts. He'd obviously just got out of bed.

'I couldn't sleep. I came down for a glass of water,' Gib said at last. 'What're you doing?'

'None of your business,' I replied. Not for the first time I wished I could think of something devastatingly cutting and witty to say. Turning back to the PC screen, I typed in the user name and password for the third time, aware that Gib had walked over to stand behind me.

Go away, I thought sullenly.

I hated people standing behind me and watching

46

what I was doing at the best of times. And this certainly wasn't the best of times.

ACCESS DENIED. PLEASE CONTACT SYSTEM MANAGER

I wasn't really surprised to see that message a third time.

'What're you doing?' Gib asked again.

Breathing deeply, I said, 'I'm trying to find out what's going on at Dad's bank.'

That was all the encouragement Gib needed. He almost ran to get a chair from around the dinner table before bringing it over and placing it right next to mine. He sat down. I scowled at him, but he didn't get the unsubtle hint. He didn't move. He fidgeted on his chair and looked away from me to the PC, but he didn't go away.

'So how's it going?' he asked, reading the screen.

'Not very well at the moment,' I said reluctantly. 'I've got as far as logging on to the bank's network but I haven't managed to log on to Dad's account to do anything yet. And I've tried three times.'

'So why can't you log on?' Gib asked.

'I . . . I think they must've disabled Dad's account. I couldn't have got the password wrong three times in a row.'

'Can't you double-check what password you *did* type in, then?' asked Gib.

I shook my head. 'When you type in a password, it doesn't show on the screen. Passwords are supposed to be secret. They wouldn't be very secret if anyone walking past your screen could see your password every time you logged on.'

'So what're you going to do now?'

'Why the sudden interest?' I couldn't help asking.

There was a pause before Gib answered.

'I want to find out what's going on just as much as you do. I want to help too,' Gib said, looking down at the carpet.

Yeah, but when I try to help, you call it crawling, I thought.

All of a sudden my eyes were stinging again. I took a deep breath and opened my eyes wide, and the stinging faded. When I was sure I wouldn't embarrass myself, I said, 'I'll log on to the computer using Dad's second account – his TEST account. He uses it for checking and testing programs. Let's hope this works.'

This time I clicked on the TEST LOGON icon.

Enter username: TEST

Enter password:

'Cross your fingers,' I said to Gib. My hands hovered over the keyboard. Please let this work, I thought desperately. If this didn't work then I'd be stuck.

I typed in the password – JABBERWOCKY44. The screen cleared. Then:

UNIVERSAL BANK DEVELOPMENT SYSTEM
THIS SYSTEM IS FOR THE EXCLUSIVE USE OF UNIVERSAL
BANK PERSONNEL. ANY UNAUTHORIZED ACCESS TO
THIS ACCOUNT MAY LEAD TO PROSECUTION.
You have 3 new mail messages
test>

appeared on the screen.

'Yeah! I'm in!' I yelled, before I remembered that Mum was upstairs.

'Shush!' Gib said urgently.

We both looked up at the ceiling. Mum and Dad's bedroom was directly above us. Anxious seconds passed as we waited. Nothing. From the sound of it, I'd got away with my outburst. There was only one explanation.

'Mum must've taken a sleeping pill.' I frowned.

'I was just about to say that,' said Gib.

I looked at Gib. He smiled at me with relief. I smiled back. Then we both remembered the evening and our smiles faded. An uncomfortable silence settled around us. I looked up at the ceiling again. Mum must have been feeling really bad to resort to taking a sleeping pill.

'Tell me what you're going to do now? Do you want me to do anything?' Gib asked.

'Er . . . I don't think so,' I replied. I turned on the printer and made sure there was plenty of paper in its paper feeder. 'Gib, you'd better make sure the door is shut properly,' I said. 'I want to print off all the inform-ation I can, so this might get noisy.'

'Noisy enough to wake Mum up?' Gib asked.

I nodded. 'You've got to make sure that she doesn't hear.'

'And just how do I do that?'

'I don't know. Think of something.'

Gib went to check the door, then came back to stand before the printer.

'How about if I put the printer on the floor?' Gib suggested. 'The carpet might muffle the sound.'

'It's worth a try.' I shrugged.

As he fiddled about with the printer, I tried to figure out what I should do next.

'I want to print out some of the staff files first. That will show us who was capable of putting the money in Dad's account,' I said. 'Then I suppose we should look at the transaction log file for yesterday . . .'

'What's in the staff file?' Gib asked, crawling under the table with the printer.

'Dad said it contains a complete description of every-one who works at the bank – their names, addresses, telephone numbers, employee numbers, departments, job descriptions and such like,' I replied. 'But I don't need all that blurb. I know what sort of person I'm looking for.'

'And what sort of person is that?' Gib asked.

'Someone who's a cashier. A cashier is the only person who could . . . No . . . that can't be right . . .' I frowned.

'What's wrong now?' asked Gib.

'Dad told me that it takes two cashiers to put money into and take money out of a bank employee's account.'

'Why two people?'

'One cashier enters all the details of a transaction, but then one of the cashier supervisors has to make sure all the details are correct before it can go any further.'

'So the same cashier can't enter the details and then double-check them?' Gib said.

'That's right.' I nodded. 'So if all that money was put into Dad's account by a cashier, then a cashier supervisor must have been in on it too.'

'Couldn't one cashier have done it on his or her own when no one else was looking?' Gib said.

I shook my head. 'Nope. The data entry account and the validation account are totally separate with two different user names and two different passwords. And Dad told me the bank has a strict policy – no one's allowed to tell anyone else their password.'

'And what exactly is this transaction log file you were talking about before?'

'Just a record of all the money coming into and going out of the bank, like Aunt Beth said. There's a new log created each night,' I replied.

51

'OK. Print out the staff file first and we'll do the other one after,' Gib suggested.

'Are you ready?' I asked. 'I'm going to display it on the screen first to make sure I can access it.'

Gib got out from under the table.

'Go ahead,' he said.

Thinking hard first, I then typed:

SHOW STAFFFILE: STAFFNAME,ADDRESS,PHONE,JOB-
DESCRIPTION,USERNAME/SORT BY STAFFNAME

'What does that mean?' Gib asked, peering over my shoulder.

'It's a database query that will display each employee's name, address, telephone number, job description and user name. If I didn't ask it for just the information I want, it would show me everything in the file and we'd be here until Christmas,' I said. The information I wanted started to appear on the screen.

Abbott, Julie: 15 Pillder Gardens: 045 2950:
    cashier Grade 2: jabbott
Amritraj, Vidal: 2 Branstep Road: 045 2379:
    programmer Grade 4: vamritraj
Andrews, Steven: 290 Eyeley Road: 056 7892:
    cashier grade 3: sandrews

I only caught the first three rows of information

before it scrolled off the screen. The file was being displayed so quickly that several screens' worth had appeared before I thought to press the <escape> key. I made sure I only pressed it once. If I pressed it twice, I'd be disconnected from the bank's network.

    test>

appeared again.

'Right. I'm going to print all this off now,' I said. I typed:

    >CREATE KEY BRIEF=STAFFNAME,ADDRESS,PHONE,
    JOBDESCRIPTION/SORT BY STAFFNAME

    >PRINT STAFFFILE/KEY=BRIEF

Immediately, the printer under the table started to rumble as the paper moved through it. Then it started to make an awful turbo-charged wheezy, screaming noise. It was really loud!

'Gib, do something!' I implored.

I looked up at the ceiling. Sleeping pill or no sleeping pill, with all this racket Mum might still come thundering down the stairs. Gib dived back under the table. He crouched over the printer, covering it with his body. It did help to muffle the sound, but the printer was still making a horrible noise.

'How long is this file?' Gib hissed.

'I don't know. But it contains the names of every person in the same office as Dad at Universal Bank so it might take a couple of minutes,' I replied.

'Minutes!' Gib protested.

He looked down at the paper coming out of the printer.

'Oh well! It's started now. We might as well leave it printing until the last possible second.'

I watched the ceiling apprehensively but there wasn't a sound from Mum and Dad's bedroom. After what seemed like three hours rather than three minutes, the printer finally stopped.

'You don't have to print anything else, do you?' Gib said.

'Just some details from the transaction log,' I answered.

Gib groaned. 'Get on with it then. I'm getting pins and needles.'

'Stop moaning!' I snapped. 'I'd rather be in bed too, you know.' I glanced across to the LED clock display on our DVD player. One-thirty in the morning!

'Do you think this transformers log file will tell us who put that money in Dad's bank account?' Gib asked, still crouching over the printer.

'Transaction log file, not transformers log file, you pillock!' I corrected.

'Whatever,' Gib dismissed. 'So will the file give us the info we need or not?'

I thought for a moment. 'I wouldn't have thought so,' I said slowly. 'The bank must already have checked that before Dad was arrested. The file probably says Dad put all that money in his account himself. But there might be some other clue in the file, that's why I want to see exactly what it says. There might be something in it that the bank has forgotten or overlooked.'

'Like what?'

'Now how should I know that?' I asked.

'It's a bit unlikely,' Gib sighed.

'I've got to start somewhere,' I replied, annoyed. I was getting precious little encouragement.

'Get on with it then.' Gib came out from under the table and shook out his arms and legs. 'My legs are going to sleep. I'll crouch over the printer when you're ready to print something.'

'All right then. Now, let me think. I want to make sure I get this right.' I was talking more to myself than to Gib. 'Besides the cashiers, who else could have put that money in Dad's account . . . ?'

'From the way Dad's always going on, I would have thought anyone who was a good enough programmer could write a program to do it,' Gib said, sitting down in his chair again. 'Isn't that why he's always talking about how difficult his job is?'

'Hhmm!' I mused. 'The thing is, if you write a new program or modify an old one, it's supposed to be compiled, linked and tested by someone else, someone

55

different, to make sure that you aren't putting cons and tricks into it. Dad said programs only get added to the overnight batch job after they've been thoroughly tested. And then there's Dad's special checking program.'

'Checking program?'

'Dad wrote most of it himself. It runs at the start of every weekend. It adds about two hours to the time it takes for the batch job to run, so they only run it on Fridays or Saturdays,' I said. 'It checks to make sure that nothing strange has happened to the batch programs during the week. Dad said nothing could get past that.'

'So what other way could it have been done?' Gib said.

'There *is* no other way. Either the money was transferred by two of the cashiers or someone wrote a program to transfer the money, which somehow got through the system without being detected,' I said. 'But if someone *did* write a program, why did they put the money into Dad's account? *Why not their own?*'

'How can we check to make sure it wasn't a program?' Gib said.

'I could print off the details of each program in the batch-job library file, I suppose,' I said doubtfully. 'That's where the details of all the programs are stored. That would tell us if any batch programs had been changed or added recently.'

'How many batch programs are there?' asked Gib.

'I think Dad said between one hundred and fifty and two hundred,' I replied with a grimace.

Gib stared at me. 'How on earth are you going to check all those? You can't know all the file names?'

I was tempted not to tell him the truth. He looked so impressed. But in the end I couldn't be bothered to wind him up.

'I don't have to know all the file names. The batch library file works just like a real library. It keeps a record of all the batch programs. It tells you when they were compiled, who changed the program and when, and some other stuff. And it keeps a record of the latest version number of each program.'

'Are you going to print out the programs as well or just what's in the batch library?'

'There's no point in my printing out the programs. I wouldn't understand them,' I admitted.

I started typing again.

```
>PRINT LIBRARY
UNIBATCH/LIST=FULL/SINCE=15MAY
```

'What does all that mean? I'm sick of asking you that all the time,' Gib complained.

'Then you should have paid attention when Dad was telling me all this,' I replied, without much sympathy. 'I've asked for a print out of all program modifications and additions made since last Monday, the fifteenth of May.'

'What's UNIBATCH?'

'That's the name of the library where all the bank's batch programs sit. I think it stands for Universal Bank batch job – or something like that,' I replied. 'Now are you going to get under the table or not?'

Muttering under his breath, Gib scooted under the table. He picked up the printer and put it in his lap before bending over it. With one last nervous look at the ceiling, I clicked on the confirm print command. Within seconds the printer had started up again.

'I'm going to get a drink,' I said, standing up.

'No, you can't,' Gib protested quickly. 'If you open that door, Mum will hear us for sure.'

I sat down again. 'This is going to take ages,' I moaned.

'At least you don't have to sit under the table, cradling the printer,' Gib snorted. 'Besides, there can't have been that many programs added or changed since Monday.'

'Maybe I should have done it for the whole of May?' I queried.

'We can always go back further if we don't find anything at first,' Gib said. 'But I think this is enough. Sitting here is cheesing me right off!'

After a couple of minutes, all the information had been printed.

'Can I stand up now?' Gib whined.

'Oh, go on then. I've only got one more thing to print off and it'll take some time to set up. I want to print off the transaction log file for yesterday. If two cashiers *did* do it then that's where we're going to find out about it.'

'Haven't we finished yet?'

'Stop whinging,' I ordered. 'You're getting on my nerves.'

Gib emerged, bending and straightening his legs to get the blood going again. I turned back to the PC screen, ready to start typing.

'Oh-oh!' I said. My heart began to hammer inside me.

'What's the matter?' Gib asked, stopping his leg exercises to look at the screen.

>MESSAGE: THIS IS THE SYSTEM OPERATOR. WHO IS USING THIS ACCOUNT? PLEASE IDENTIFY YOURSELF.
>MESSAGE:

'Do something!' Gib said urgently. 'You're not supposed to be on the bank's computer. Vicky, do something. Log off.'

I didn't even bother to log off. I clicked on the icon for the router that allowed me to get onto the Internet, then clicked on the option to turn it off. It must have taken me about a second and a half.

appeared on the screen. I quickly switched off the PC.

'Will they know it was us?' Gib asked anxiously.

'I'm not sure. I think all the operators would've been able to see was that someone had logged on to the TEST account. But hopefully I disconnected us from the Internet before they could trace us.'

'Are you sure?'

I shook my head. I wasn't sure at all.

'Great,' Gib fumed. 'We can't help Dad if we're arrested too.'

'We won't be. They can't prove it was us,' I replied, faking confidence.

'You don't know that for certain,' Gib pointed out.

'Well, we'll soon find out,' I said. 'If they do know it's us, they'll do something about it.'

'Like what, for example?' Gib asked quietly.

'Like call the police,' I replied.

Chapter Five

Getting it Wrong

It only took Gib and me a couple of minutes to get back to our bedrooms. Gib said that he'd take the print-outs upstairs with him and I didn't argue. I went into my room, switched off the light and got into bed – but I didn't even try to sleep. I knew that it would be impossible. How could I sleep when the police might knock on the door at any second?

'Please, *please* don't let the police arrive,' I prayed into the darkness.

I was scared for myself, but I was more terrified about what it might do to Mum. How would she take it if Gib and I were arrested too? I tried to tell myself that it was just my imagination rushing about at warp speed, but it didn't help.

'Don't panic, Victoria,' I told myself. 'Think of something else.' But what?

I waited for something slight and silly to pop into my head. Nothing arrived.

Come on, Victoria Gibson, I thought sternly. Don't

you dare panic. You won't help anyone by panicking. Victoria . . . Everyone called me Vicky – except Dad and Mrs Bracken. I preferred Victoria to Vicky. Vicky sounded like something you stuffed up your nose when you had a cold, but I'd never told anyone that. I didn't want people to think I was trying to be grand or something, because I wasn't. But Victoria was such a grand name. VIC-TOR-EEE-AH!

And I knew why I was called Victoria too. One of my real mum and dad's friends had told the social worker who had told my current mum and dad.

I wasn't called Victoria after Queen Victoria or even because anyone felt particularly victorious at having me. I was called Victoria because I was almost born there. At Victoria Station. My real mum and dad had just stepped off the Orpington train when my mum started getting labour pains. Some quick-minded person called an ambulance and Mum only just made it to Westminster Hospital in time to have me. And Victoria was a better name than Westminster!

I can't remember my real mum and dad at all. I didn't like admitting that to myself, but it was true. They had gone off for a weekend's holiday. Their first holiday since I was born. They were on the last day of the holiday when the accident happened. I was only a few weeks old when they drowned. They were in a hired boat when a sudden squall blew up. They'd left me with friends until they got back – only they never got back.

They had died. I hadn't. That made me feel strange, guilty – like somehow Mum and Dad dying was my fault in some way. Like maybe it was somehow wrong for me to live when they'd died.

It was as Gib said – they had needed to get away from me . . .

I thought about the only photo I had of my real mum and dad. It was taken at their wedding. I'd put it back in my top drawer under my socks and I was that close to taking it out again. I didn't look at it very often – it made me feel funny peculiar. It was a good photo though. Mum and Dad were smiling at the camera and they looked so happy. I usually only took it out to look at when I felt happy too, but earlier I'd needed to look at them. I'd needed to remember that I had belonged once, to people who'd cared about me.

They'd wanted me . . . except for the weekend when they went away on holiday . . . maybe . . .

Mum and Dad had given up all hope of having any children of their own, so they fostered me practically as soon as my real parents died. Then Mum number two discovered she was three months pregnant. They kept me though and, after a year, they adopted me. So I'm only a few months older than Gib. I'm one of the oldest in my year, Gib's one of the youngest. He acts it too!

My second mum and dad told me that I was extra-special.

'Not only have you had two sets of parents rather than one . . .' Dad began.

'But you were chosen by us rather than born to us the way your brother was,' Mum finished.

That had made me feel good. I was chosen. With Gib they'd had to take what they got!

Thinking about Gib began to make me sad as well as double-worried. Even after what he'd said, I still thought of him as my brother. His real name is Richard but a couple of years ago, he got everyone to call him Gib. I once asked him what was wrong with Richard.

'There's no way I'm going to let people call us Ricky and Vicky. Yuk! Double and triple yuk!' he told me.

Gib looks like Dad. They both have short black hair and the darkest brown eyes I've ever seen. Mum's hair is really peculiar. She calls it Titian red. Dad's always teasing her that it looks more like milky-tea brown to him! She has dark green eyes, the exact same colour as oak-tree leaves.

As for me, well, I have black hair and dark brown eyes and good teeth with only one filling in my entire mouth. I'm proud of that. Gib's got more metal in his mouth than in the whole of Dad's car.

Please don't let the police come for us.

The thought sneaked into my head. Frowning, I turned over to lie on my side. Closing my eyes, I tried to think of only good things. I thought about my teeth. I thought about Mum and Dad and our trip to Scotland last year. I counted all the good things I could remember instead of counting sheep. And it worked. The panicky feeling began to fade. My eyelids felt heavy. I counted more good things: playing tennis for the school team; the way my friend Gayle made me laugh; Mr Jackson, my English teacher . . .

The next thing I knew, it was morning. And a horribly bright, sunny morning at that. The sort of morning when things should've been all right instead of all wrong.

After my shower, I went down for breakfast. Mum and Gib were already downstairs. Gib and I exchanged a look of relief before I turned to Mum. No police! We'd got away with it.

Mum had on her shoes instead of her slippers and already had one arm inside her jacket.

'I'm off to the court now,' she said to no one in particular. 'I don't know when I'll be back. I've left twenty pounds on the dinner table. Both of you can have a pizza for lunch if I'm not back in time.'

'Can't we come with you, Mum?' I asked.

A part of me was curious. I'd never been in a courtroom before. But more than that I wanted to see Dad. I wanted to tell him how Gib and I were trying to help him. And seeing him would reassure me that he was all right. I was already missing him dreadfully.

'No, dear,' Mum replied. 'Your dad doesn't think a courtroom is the place for you and Gib, and I agree.

Besides, he'll probably be in and out of the court in ten minutes. You'll see him this evening when he comes home.'

As I opened my mouth to argue, I felt a sharp pain in my shin. Gib had kicked me under the table. I gave him a filthy look, but I did get the message. I shut up.

'Now where on earth is my taxi?' Mum muttered. She sipped at her cup of decaffeinated coffee, then frowned at the kitchen clock.

The doorbell rang. Mum put her coffee cup down, then glanced down at her watch.

'On time – for a change!' she said, impressed.

We followed her out into the hall. Mum opened the door. Sunlight streamed into the hall, despite the two men standing at the door. My heart stopped beating as I recognized the man wearing black jeans and a blue shirt, open at the neck. It was Eric Jones, the Systems Manager in charge of all the computer operators at Dad's bank. He'd sometimes come round our house for dinner, and Mum and Dad had been to his thirty-fifth birthday party. The other man I didn't recognize. He wore heavy-rimmed glasses and blinked a lot. He had on jeans and a clean red T-shirt. Both of them looked serious, almost stern. I looked at Gib. He looked at me. I held my breath.

'Hello, Laura,' Eric said quietly. 'This is Patrick, one of my operators.'

'Hello, Eric, Patrick,' Mum said, surprised. 'What brings you here?'

Eric winced and looked totally uncomfortable.

'I . . . I'm sorry, Laura, but . . . well, we've got orders to take back your PC.'

'I beg your pardon,' Mum said slowly.

I could see her lips thinning and her eyes getting hard.

'We've . . . we've been told not to leave without it,' Eric said apologetically.

'And just why should you want the PC back? Isn't my husband, David, innocent until proven guilty or have Universal Bank already made up their minds?' Mum said angrily.

'We're just following orders,' Eric began, but at the look on Mum's face he shut up.

'Why the intense hurry to get the PC back?' Mum asked, still fuming.

Eric and Patrick looked at each other.

'I think the bank felt it was . . . advisable, Mrs Gibson,' Patrick said slowly.

Mistake!

'Advisable! And just what does that mean? Advis . . .' Mum had saddled her high horse and was off at a gallop now.

'Laura, it's for your own protection in a way,' Eric interrupted. 'You see, last night I was logged on to my SYSTEM account and someone with a remote PC dialled

67

into the bank's computer. They logged on to the TEST account which is used by a number of people and logged off before we could get the IP address, so we have no way of knowing who it was. Luckily for us, they logged on to the development machine rather than the live machine, so no harm was done, but—'

'And you think it was me . . .'

I thought Mum was going to explode.

'Mum, you're not supposed to get upset – remember?' Gib said, taking the words out of my mouth.

Mum took a deep breath, then another.

'I'll have you know, I barely know how to switch on the wretched thing, much less log on to Universal's computer. And I resent the implication,' Mum said. Her voice was now steadier but icy.

'No one's accusing you, Laura.' Eric raised a placating hand.

'You could've fooled me,' Mum said. 'Or maybe you're blaming my children now? Go on – confess, Vicky! You got up at three o'clock in the morning to break into Universal's computer, and Gib was there helping you!'

My face was burning. I looked at Gib and we both looked down at our feet.

'We're just doing our job, Mrs Gibson,' Patrick said.

'I'm sorry but we do have to take the PC back with us, Laura,' Eric continued. 'I tried to argue against it but the General Manager wasn't having any. That's why I came here personally, even though I shouldn't have. I didn't want operators you didn't know knocking on your door. We're friends and I didn't want you to feel that I'd turned my back on you. I'm doing everything I can from my end to prove that David had nothing to do with that money appearing in his account.'

'Take the PC then. And be quick about it,' Mum ordered. 'Vicky, show these *gentlemen* where your dad keeps it.'

'But, Mum, they can't take the PC,' I protested. 'I use it for my computing homework. What—?'

'You'll just have to do without,' Mum interrupted. 'I wouldn't keep that thing in my house if Universal Bank begged me.'

Reluctantly, Gib and I led the way into the living room. I pointed to the PC, then turned away. I couldn't bear to watch. It was like watching one of my arms or legs being taken away. Dad hadn't bothered buying one of our own as the one the bank gave him was more than enough for all of us to use.

This was disastrous. How was I supposed to get back on to the bank's computer when I didn't even have a PC to use? And all those listings we'd printed out – they were absolutely useless. By mistake I'd logged on to the *development* system rather than the live system. Like a fool, I'd forgotten that the TEST account was on the development system where all the programs were written and tested.

Everyone at the bank – except the programmers – had an account on the live machine. The programmers' finished programs were automatically copied across from the development system to the live one, but only when they'd been thoroughly tested by acceptance testers first. The thing was, for the money to be put into Dad's account, it had to be done from the live system, so everything Gib and I had done during the night had been an utter waste of time. And, looking at Gib, I knew he realized it too.

Patrick carried the printer with the screen on top of it, while Eric put the keyboard on top of the PC processor. Then he saw the storage case that contained Dad's memory sticks and the writeable CDs he'd burned.

'You can't take those. Dad bought them with his own money,' I said vehemently. 'They don't belong to your rotten bank. And they've got my homework on. Take your eyes off them.'

'Vicky, I am sorry.' Eric tried to smile at me but it didn't come off. He looked only slightly less unhappy than I felt. 'Believe me, I know your dad is innocent of this. I'm doing everything I can. I promise.'

'Yeah, of course you are,' Gib scorned. 'We can see that.'

Eric's face flushed a slow red.

'Just don't touch our private stuff,' I said through gritted teeth.

Both men looked doubtfully from the disks to me, but it worked. They didn't take them. It was stupid, I knew. CDs and memory keys wouldn't be much good without a PC, but all I could think about was that the bank shouldn't take everything back. Gib and I followed the men into the hall and watched as they left the house.

'You go on ahead, Patrick. I'll catch you up,' Eric said.

We all watched as Patrick walked out to their car, parked in front of our house.

'I'm sorry, Laura. I really am,' Eric said softly. 'But I want you to know I'm doing all I can to clear David. I'm almost sure he had nothing to do with this business.'

'Well, we *know* he's innocent for a fact,' Gib interjected.

'Gib . . .' Mum warned. 'Thanks, Eric.'

She was still furious. Eric walked out of the house and Mum . . . well, she didn't exactly slam the door shut but she did close it really hard. The doorbell rang again almost immediately.

'If they've forgotten anything, then tough,' Mum mumbled.

She opened the door. A tall woman with short hair stood halfway down our garden path.

'Did someone here order a taxi?' the woman asked. Behind her I could see Eric and Patrick getting into their car.

'Yes, I did,' Mum replied. 'I'll be right with you.'

She turned to us. It took her a few seconds to remember how to smile.

'You two be good. I'll see you later.'

'Be careful, Mum,' I said, 'and send Dad our love.'

Mum nodded, then left the house. I turned to Gib.

'I logged on to the wrong system and wasted all that time and now we don't even have a PC to do it again,' I sighed.

'Then we'll just have to find another PC to use.'

'And where do we find one? They don't grow on trees, you know,' I snapped. But I was more annoyed with myself than with Gib. I felt like a complete twerp. 'Well? Where do . . . ?'

'Internet Café!' he said smugly. 'They've got loads of PCs – and it just costs a quid or something.'

'Oh great!' I retorted. 'You want us to hack into a bank's computer using a public PC in a café, whilst the police and MI5 and God knows who else monitors what we do?'

'Oh,' said Gib, deflated.

I left him chewing his lip and went to get my breakfast. But once I'd put the Weetabix in my bowl, I wasn't hungry any more.

'Vicky! VICKY! I've got it!' Gib came running into the kitchen.

'Don't give it to me then,' I replied.

Puzzled, Gib looked at me. He smiled, then he frowned.

'This is serious, Vicky,' he said. 'I know where there's a PC we can use.'

'I'm listening.'

'Chaucy's got one.'

I groaned inwardly. 'Don't you know anyone else who owns a PC?' I asked.

'Chaucy's is state of the art,' Gib answered.

'I don't want to use Chaucy's PC,' I admitted.

'Why not?' Gib asked, surprised.

' 'Cause I don't like him,' I said honestly.

Gib looked at me. 'It's Chaucy's machine or nothing. Unless you know someone else who's got a proper PC that can go on the Internet. And someone we trust . . . I trust, who'll let us do what we want for as long as we want – no questions asked.'

I sighed. 'No, I don't,' I replied.

'Then I don't see that we've got much choice,' Gib said.

I couldn't argue with him. 'Will he let us use his PC?' I asked.

'I don't see why not. Hang on. I'll phone him and ask.'

Before I could say another word, Gib was at the phone. I went back into the living room. The table where the PC had been now looked incredibly bare. Although Dad dusted the table regularly, a fine film of dust formed the outline of where the PC and the modem had sat.

'Vicky, where are you?' Gib bellowed.

I went out into the hall. Gib was no longer on the phone.

'That was fast,' I said. 'And there's no need to shout. I'm not deaf.'

'Never mind that,' Gib dismissed. 'Chaucy's at home and he says we can use his PC any time we want to.'

'Are you sure he said "we" and not "you"?' I asked with suspicion.

'He definitely said "we",' Gib said impatiently, adding, 'Mind you, we're probably being a bit previous, asking to use his PC. I bet we don't need to use it. I bet the magistrate throws Dad's case out. Anyone with half an eye could see Dad wouldn't do such a thing.'

'So what do we do?' I asked.

'We wait for Dad to come home first,' Gib said slowly. 'There's no point in doing anything else until he gets back. We have to find out what's going on.'

He didn't say anything else. He didn't have to. Neither of us wanted to discuss what would happen if Dad *didn't* come home . . .

Waiting for Mum and Dad to come home was the hardest waiting I'd ever had to do in my life. Gib and I couldn't find anything much to say to each other. It was as if a high wall had sprung up between us. A wall we couldn't get over or under or around. For the first time, I felt uncomfortable just being with Gib. And I didn't need my glasses to see that he felt the same way.

74

I spent the rest of the morning wandering around the house, looking for something to do to take my mind off Mum and Dad. The minute hand of my watch had never moved slower. I tried reading a book of science fiction short stories but the words kept bouncing off my head rather than sinking in. I took my book and ambled out of the house into the garden. Lunchtime had come and gone but I wasn't the least bit hungry. I'd been in the garden about fifteen minutes when Gib caught up with me. He was still wearing the same faded, grubby jeans he'd worn that morning, but he'd changed his blue shirt for the T-shirt I'd picked out with Mum for his last birthday. The T-shirt had a Superman emblem on it. I wondered why he'd bothered to change. What was wrong with the shirt he'd been wearing?

In his hands he carried the listings we'd got from the bank's development system.

'Vicky, can I go through these batch-job reports with you? I want to make sure I understand them.'

'They're not from the live system,' I frowned.

'Are the reports we get from the live system going to be that much different?' Gib asked.

I thought about it. 'I don't know. I guess not. The two systems are supposed to be identical so that programs written and tested on the development machine can be run on the live machine.'

'That's what I thought.' Gib smiled. 'So we can always treat this as a . . . a dress rehearsal, just in case.'

'I thought you wanted to wait until Dad came home before doing anything else.'

'I did, but all this waiting around is driving me crazy,' Gib replied. 'So come on, explain what this lot means.'

Gib plonked the pages of listings down on my lap. To tell the truth, I didn't want to talk to Gib. I didn't want to talk to anyone. I wanted to be by myself until Dad came home. If Dad came home . . .

Don't even think such a thing, I thought angrily.

'Dad will be back today. You just wait and see,' Gib said from beside me.

I was amazed. I turned to him, shading my eyes against the afternoon sun.

'How did you know what I was thinking?'

' 'Cause I'm your . . . because it's written all over your face,' Gib said, looking down at the ground.

Why did I get the feeling that he'd changed his mind about what he was really going to say?

'All right then,' I said reluctantly. 'I guess I've nothing better to do anyway. I'll tell you what each column means and then I'll leave you to it.'

Gib opened the listing to the first page.

'Got a pen?' I asked.

After a quick search through his trouser pockets, Gib took out a pencil. Gib's pockets were worse than Mum's handbag. They were always filled with all kinds of junk. I was sure Gib thought of his pockets as the equivalent of Batman's utility belt.

'Right then,' I began as we pored over the listings together. 'The first column is the program name, then you've got the date and time when the program was first created, the date and time when it was compiled to create an object file . . . let me see, the next column is the date and time when the object file was linked. Then you've got the user identification of the last person to change the program, followed by . . .'

'Hang on a minute,' Gib complained. 'I don't write shorthand.'

I waited for him to catch up.

'What do you mean by the program being compiled and linked?' Gib asked, writing furiously. 'And what's this object file?'

I sighed. 'There are three steps to running a program on the bank's system. First you have to write it, using an editor to produce a source program. Then you have to run a program called a COMPILER to translate the source program so that the computer can understand it. The file that holds the translation is the object file. And then all the object files have to get linked up together to produce a master program you can run on the system. With me so far?'

'Don't be snotty!' Gib ordered. 'Why not just translate the program and run it?'

'I asked Dad that. He said compiling programs takes ages. And if you did that, all the code would have to be in one file. The system at the bank must have millions and millions of lines of code and if you only wanted to change one line or one small thing, you'd still have to compile the whole lot again. So the programs are split into manageable chunks for different teams to work on and then each bit can be changed and translated separately. And then you can just link the whole lot together at the end. I think that's right.'

'Oh, I see. Then . . .'

'Hello, Gib, hello, Vicky.'

It was Mum.

I jumped up, the listings on my lap falling on to the grass. I looked past Mum eagerly. But I couldn't see Dad.

Where was he?

Chapter Six

Mr Guy and his Killer Dog

'Mum! I didn't hear you arrive. Where's Dad? Is he with you?'

Gib's questions came thick and fast. I hung back behind him – I don't know why.

'Your dad's upstairs. He's having a bath,' Mum replied.

Mum's face looked so strange. Gaunt and lean, as if in a few hours she had lost all the flesh from her cheeks. And she looked so tired. At any second she might keel over.

'What happened, Mum?' Gib asked earnestly. 'Is it all over? Is it all sorted out?'

'I wish! Your dad has to give up his passport. They want to make sure he doesn't skip the country with the bank's supposed million,' Mum said bitterly. 'Once a date for the trial is set then he'll have to appear in court again.'

'But at least he's home now,' I said.

'But at least he's home,' Mum agreed.

I watched as she leaned against the door, her chin against her chest.

'Now, I want you two to promise me something. I don't want either of you to say a word about this business to your dad. Not one single word. Do you understand?'

I nodded.

'Yes, Mum,' Gib said, adding, 'Can we see Dad? Is he all right?'

'He's fine. He wants to see you after his bath. Then I want him to get some sleep. He's very tired.'

'Mum . . . what's going to happen about Dad's job?' I couldn't help asking. 'I mean . . . will he be able to clear his name when he gets back to work on Monday?'

'He's been suspended from work until the outcome of the trial is known,' Mum said, her voice as hard as granite. 'Eric, the Systems Manager, said he'd try to help us and I know Beth will do what she can. We'll just have to keep our fingers crossed that they find something.' And with that, Mum went back into the house.

After she'd gone, the garden, the whole world was silent. No birds, no traffic, no nothing. At least, if there were sounds then I couldn't hear them. There was just Gib and me staring after her. I forced myself to break the silence.

'We're going to need Chaucy's PC,' I said softly.

'I was just thinking that,' Gib said, without looking at me. 'I'll go and check it out.'

We both went into the house. I went upstairs to my

room. I waited by my bedroom door until I heard Dad emerging from the bathroom, then I ran out on to the landing. Dad had on his white towelling dressing gown and his back was towards me as he closed the bathroom door.

'Dad, I . . .'

Whatever else I'd wanted to say vanished out of my head when I saw him. I'd thought Mum looked bad. But Dad looked far, far worse. All the life and laughter had gone from his face. Only as soon as he saw me, he tried to smile. He straightened up and ran his hand over his damp hair.

'Hello, Victoria. Good grief! It feels like I haven't seen you in weeks rather than just one day,' Dad said, holding out his arms.

I walked into them and he hugged me. I nodded slowly.

'How are you?' he asked.

I nodded again.

'You're very quiet, pumpkin,' Dad smiled.

That did it! My eyes started to leak and I was off again. I covered my face with my hands, too upset to be embarrassed, too miserable to care. The next thing I knew, Dad was smoothing down my hair and sighing.

'Victoria, don't cry,' he said soothingly. 'I'm all right, I promise. And this thing will never get to trial. The bank will find out before then that I didn't take the money.'

'How will they find out?' I sniffed.

'I may have been suspended, but I still have friends at the bank,' Dad replied.

'Like Aunt Beth and Eric?' I asked.

'That's right.' Dad smiled. 'Eric's a good Systems Manager and Beth knows her way around most of the programs on the system. Between the two of them they should be able to find out something that'll help me.'

'D'you really think so?' I asked.

Dad nodded.

'How ... how did that money get into your account?' I whispered.

Dad's smile faded. 'Well, if I knew that, I'd be halfway towards solving this mystery.'

I wiped my eyes with the back of my hand, feeling better now that we were talking about it.

'Why should anyone want to put that million in your account? That's what I can't understand,' I complained.

Dad nodded. 'If I knew that then I'd be three-quarters of the way towards solving the mystery.'

'And the last quarter?' I asked.

Dad's face was stony. 'Finding out who did all this.'

'Do you have any idea who that might be?'

'That's just it, I don't. Nothing definite at any rate,' Dad sighed. 'And even if I did know for sure who it was, that wouldn't help. I need proof. Concrete, indisputable proof.'

I looked at Dad. Neither of us spoke for a few moments.

'Proof that someone else is guilty to prove that you're innocent,' I said slowly.

'Exactly. Right now I don't see how I can prove my innocence otherwise.'

'Dad . . .'

'Enough questions, Victoria. All I want to do now is sleep for a week,' Dad said.

Mum came out of their bedroom. She glared at me. I'd forgotten what she'd said in the garden. When Dad went into their bedroom, Mum looked at me and shook her head.

'Oh, Vicky,' she sighed, before following Dad into the room and closing the door behind her.

I chewed on my bottom lip, feeling about two centimetres high. I had a pain in my chest and my throat felt as if it was full of sand.

Unwanted again.

I moved towards the door, ready to knock and say sorry. I hadn't done it deliberately. I'd just forgotten.

'David, I'm sorry. I asked Vicky not to mention the bank.' I heard Mum's muffled voice through the closed door. I grimaced at her words, feeling worse than terrible.

'Why not?' Dad asked. 'I'm glad she wanted to talk about it. It's better than what everyone else is doing. Skirting around the subject but still dying to know all the ins and outs and in-betweens.'

'But I don't want you upset any more by this business,' Mum said.

'You're the one who shouldn't get upset, Laura. It's you I'm worried about,' Dad replied.

I didn't mean to listen, but my feet had forgotten how to move.

'D'you know what burns me up about this whole thing?' Dad said, his voice louder with anger now. 'If I was some smart-alec hacker from outside who'd been accused of taking the money, the bank would be doing their best to keep all this quiet. They'd probably even let me keep the money as long as I told them how I did it!'

'David!' Mum interrupted.

'Oh, all right! Maybe that's not quite true,' Dad replied. 'But what gets me is that I work at the bank and so I must be guilty. They even think they know how I did it. Beth told me they reckon I set something up in my checking software. So it's David Gibson off to prison, and throw away the key. But I didn't do it. I DIDN'T DO IT! I'm so angry I want to hit something.'

'I know, David,' Mum soothed. 'Calm down, dear.'

'I can't,' Dad sighed. 'I've been caught in a trap and if I'm not careful I'll end up in prison with no one but you and the kids giving a damn about me.'

I walked away after that. I couldn't bear to listen to any more. I trudged downstairs and out into the garden, feeling very scared.

★ ★ ★

'Vicky, I've been looking for you all over the house,' Gib moaned as soon as he saw me.

'You should have looked out here then,' I replied, not bothering to look up from the listings Gib and I had been going through earlier and that I was looking at now.

It was late evening. The sun was getting low in the burnt orange-red sky and the garden was still and peaceful. Usually on Saturday evenings I went around to Gayle's or Maggie's house. We'd go to see a film or go on a pizza crawl, but today I hadn't felt like it. I'd spent the whole afternoon thinking and reading through the listings.

'We can't use Chaucy's PC,' Gib said, flopping down beside me.

'Why not?' I frowned at Gib. 'Won't he let us use it? Did he change his mind?'

'No, it's not that,' Gib sighed. 'Once I'd explained to him why we needed it, Chaucy said we could use it whenever we wanted to. But he said his router is playing up so we've got no way of getting onto the Internet to connect to the Universal Bank computer.'

'You didn't tell Chaucy the whole truth, did you?' I asked, shocked.

Gib frowned at me. 'Of course I did. Why not? He's my friend. He won't tell anyone.'

'But . . . but . . .'

Just thinking that Chaucy knew about Dad made me

go cold all over. It would be just another thing for Chaucy to grin at me about.

'You had no right to tell Chaucy our business,' I said furiously.

Gib's frown deepened. 'Listen, Chaucy's my friend, not yours. I'll tell him what I like.'

'And Dad is your real dad not mine, so this whole thing is none of my business,' I concluded. I hadn't meant to say that – I swear. It just slipped out.

'I didn't say that,' Gib said quietly.

'But that's what you meant – if I remember yester-day's little speech correctly.'

My voice was lemon-bitter. Now that it had been brought out into the open, I couldn't get it out of my mind. I had no real aunts and uncles. Just some very distant cousins who lived in America whom I'd never even seen. My close relatives were those I'd acquired when I'd been adopted. Neither my real mum nor my real dad had any brothers and sisters. And now, more than ever, I wished with all my heart that they did. I'd never felt so lonely. Picking up the listings I went indoors.

'So what now, Victoria?' I asked myself. I sat down on the sofa in the living room and leaned my head back, trying to think. It seemed to me that no matter what I did, Gib would never accept me. I'd never be a part of *his* family.

But if I prove Dad didn't take that money then I'll

belong. Then Dad will want me to stay and maybe Mum too, I thought. I mean, that wouldn't be my only reason for wanting to prove it, but it could be one of them.

But now I wasn't even sure if I wanted to belong. Much as I loved Mum and Dad, they'd never be my *real* mum and dad.

Did that matter? Surely it was up to me to decide where I fitted in? If I said the Gibsons were my family, who could contradict me? The opinion of anyone outside the family wasn't – what was the word? – relevant. And as for the family's opinion? Well, Mum and Dad *had* adopted me. No one had forced them to do that.

So there was just Gib.

'Think of something else, Victoria,' I told myself.

What was it Dad always said? Every problem has a logical solution? Well, I couldn't see the solution to this one to save my life. When one or two things went wrong it was so easy to think that nothing would go right. I'd have to have it out with Gib, once this business at the bank was sorted out. But my luck was non-existent even as far as that was concerned. I needed a PC with an Internet connection. It was that simple. Only Dad's PC had been taken away and Chaucy couldn't get onto the Web. So where could I find what I needed? There were plenty of PCs at school that would allow me to go online, of course. But short of breaking into the school, how could I get to them?

Short of breaking into the school . . .

I sat up abruptly. I couldn't . . . *could I*? I didn't see that I had much choice. It was that or nothing. I knew Dad said Aunt Beth and Eric and others were helping him at the bank, but what if they couldn't? They all knew more about computing than I did, but I couldn't just sit by and watch Dad end up in prison. Not without doing something to help. The way I saw it, I couldn't *hurt* anything by trying to prove Dad was innocent.

But breaking into school?

'Does that mean you're not going to help Dad any more?' Gib was standing at the living-room door.

Wishing he'd leave me alone, I snapped, 'It doesn't mean anything of the kind.'

'How are you going to get the information you need from the live system at Universal Bank?' Gib asked.

'I've thought of a way – a possible way,' I said slowly.

Silence.

'Aren't you going to tell me?' Gib frowned.

'I'm not sure. It's dangerous. It'd be better if you didn't know. There's no point in both of us getting into trouble.'

'I'm part of this too,' Gib said angrily.

'Shush!' I said, pointing to the ceiling. I didn't want to disturb Dad.

'So what's your plan?'

I looked at Gib, wondering if I dared tell him.

'We use a school PC,' I replied.

Gib stared at me.

'When?'

'No time like the present,' I said.

Gib glanced down at his watch and frowned.

'But it's almost eight o'clock. School's locked up!'

'Like I said, you don't have to help me with this.' I stood up, picked up the storage case with Dad's CDs and memory keys in it and pushed past Gib into the hall. I put on my jacket.

'I'm coming with you,' Gib whispered. 'You don't think I'd let you do this by yourself, do you?'

'Scribble a quick note to Mum and Dad telling them we've gone to see a film or something and let's go,' I ordered.

Gib opened his mouth to argue, then shut it again. It was just as well. I was really in the mood for an argument at that moment!

It was only when we were actually on the way to our school that I began to believe what we were about to do.

'When there's no traffic around, I'll help you climb over the school railings,' Gib told me as we approached the road where our school was.

'Help me? It's more likely that I'll be the one helping you,' I scoffed. 'Besides, we might not have to climb over anything.'

'Of course we will. The gates will be locked on a Saturday,' Gib replied.

'Supposing we're seen . . .' I began.

'We just have to make sure we're not seen,' Gib interrupted.

'I was just going to say, we'd better have our story straight,' I continued impatiently.

'All right then,' Gib said. 'You've left something in your locker and we want it, *need* it before Monday.'

'Like what?' I asked.

'I dunno. A present for Mum.'

'Why have I got her a present? It's not her birthday.'

'You're not helping much, Vicky,' Gib complained, his arms folded.

'All right! All right! We'll say that then,' I conceded. 'But Mum's present is in your locker, not mine. I've got quite enough on my plate at the moment, what with Miss Hiff's letter about the "Hacker Supreme".'

'Oh yeah . . . I'd forgotten about that,' Gib replied.

'I hadn't.'

We walked in silence around the corner of the road. Boroughvale was at the other end of the street.

'I reckon the best place to get over the railings is behind the goal posts. There's practically no hedge left there. It's been battered too much by us getting the balls back that missed the goal.'

A privet hedge stood between the school fields and buildings and the railings which ran at least two-thirds of the way around the school boundary.

'Will you be able to lift me?' I asked Gib doubtfully.

'Of course I can.' Gib sounded insulted. 'And once we're in, I've got my torch and some string and some sweets if we should get stuck there overnight . . .

'What's the string for?' I asked.

'I thought we could tie it to a railing and use it to find our way out of school.'

'But that's what the torch is for,' I said, getting confused. 'And besides, we could both find our way out of school with blindfolds on. We come here every day – remember?'

'But we *might* need the string. Anything might happen. I might drop the torch and break it,' Gib said.

I burst out laughing. 'Don't get carried away, Gib. We're not going to get stuck until morning and you're *not* going to drop your torch.'

'OK!' Gib pouted, the tops of his ears a brilliant red. 'That still leaves one problem though.'

'Yes, I know,' I said gloomily.

Neither of us had to say it. We both knew. Mr Guy, the caretaker, and his killer dog, Jaws.

Not that any of us had actually seen Jaws. Mr Guy was always telling us that Jaws had to be kept chained up inside the caretaker's house during the day for our own protection. Well, if the dog was half as bad as Mr Guy, it would be a right snarling misery. A Rottweiler or at the very least a great hulking brute of an Alsatian. Would Jaws be roaming around the school, ready to bite our legs off when he got the first sniff of us?

'I don't suppose you've come up with a master plan for dealing with the dog?' I asked.

'Ah, that's where you're wrong. Yes, I have,' Gib replied smugly.

'I'm all ears,' I prompted.

'If we see Jaws or hear him or even just suspect he's near by we do one simple thing.'

'What?'

'Run!'

I looked at Gib and we both cracked up laughing.

'You must have racked your brains all the way here to come up with that one!' I said.

At last we reached our school. What an anticlimax! The gate was wide open and it seemed as if every light in the place was on.

'So much for my torch,' Gib said, disappointed.

'And so much for climbing the railings,' I said, not disappointed.

The smile on my face was so broad it almost hurt. 'I forgot about the adult education classes that go on here.'

'Hmm!' Gib snorted. He was really annoyed. Pin-head!

We both strolled into the school. We passed the canteen first. It was full of people who completely ignored us. Next, up the steps and along the quad and past the assembly hall. Just then, a small cocker spaniel came trotting up to us.

'Hello, boy,' I smiled, bending to fuss behind its ears. 'Who do you belong to then?'

'Jaws! JAWS! Here, boy!' Mr Guy came trotting up behind his dog. This was Jaws! I couldn't believe my eyes – or my ears.

Mr Guy glared over his glasses at me and Gib. He had on dark slacks and a light-blue polo shirt. His bald head gleamed like a snooker ball. And Jaws, who barely came up past my ankle, was sniffing and yapping at my feet. We couldn't help it. Gib and I laughed so hard, he was holding his side and I had tears in my eyes.

''Ere! I know you two,' Mr Guy said, not amused. 'You two come to school here during the day, don't you? I'm sure I've seen you knocking about. So what are you doing here now then?'

And that question wiped the smile right off our faces.

Chapter Seven

The Dictionary Dodge

'This is Vicky and I'm Gib,' Gib said quickly.

I could have kicked him. What on earth was he doing giving Mr Guy our names? Trying to get us both expelled?

'So what are you doing here then?' asked Mr Guy again, picking up his killer dog.

'Our mum is doing an evening class here and we said we'd meet her,' Gib replied.

I held my breath as I watched Mr Guy. I was going to keep well out of this one. The caretaker frowned and glanced down at his watch, almost tipping Jaws out of his arms.

'But evening classes don't finish for another hour and a bit yet,' he said.

'Yeah, we know,' Gib smiled. 'Maybe you could tell us where we can find her. What classroom is the computing course going on in?'

'Science block. Room Twenty-four,' Mr Guy said.

'Can you come with us?' Gib asked.

I gasped, then quickly tried to conceal it with a weak smile. Have you lost your mind? I thought, forcing myself not to glare at Gib. I looked up at Mr Guy, trying to keep the panic off my face.

'You must be bloomin' joking. Do I look like I've got nothing better to do than traipse around the school after you two?' frowned Mr Guy. 'You know where the science block is as well as I do. Now shift.'

Gib grabbed me and pulled me along to the science block.

'What on earth did you do that for?' I hissed. 'Are you crazy? Suppose he'd decided to come with us?'

'I knew he wouldn't.' Gib shrugged calmly. 'The only reason he'd come with us was if he thought we didn't want him to.'

I shook my head at Gib, impressed and yet horrified at his nerve.

'One of these days that mouth of yours isn't going to be quite so quick and it's going to get you into a lot of trouble,' I said.

'Or it's going to be too quick and it'll be the same result,' Gib said dryly.

'The way you can lie without batting an eyelid! How do you do it? Practice?'

'You're being snotty again!' Gib sniffed. 'Besides I don't usually tell lies unless it's for a good reason. And this is the best.'

95

'And what happens if Mr Guy tells one of our teachers that we were here tonight?' I asked.

'You worry too much.' Gib shrugged. 'We'll just say we were here to meet our mum like we told Mr Guy. No big deal.'

'Hmm!' I still wasn't convinced.

We entered the science block and walked up to the second floor to get to Room 24. We peered though the glass panel in the door. A tall, skinny black woman wearing a dark-blue trouser-suit was the only one in the room. She was bustling around from table to table.

'Here goes.' Gib said what I was thinking.

I knocked on the door and Gib and I walked into the classroom. The woman straightened up when she saw us.

'Hi,' she said.

'Hi,' Gib replied.

I just smiled.

Silence.

'I'm Rosa, the tutor,' she said when it was obvious we weren't about to carry on. 'Can I help you?'

'We come to this school during the day,' I said, for want of something better to say.

'Is that so?'

'I . . . that is . . . we . . .' I stammered.

'Can we ask you for a favour?' Gib said. He managed to sound both keen and desperate at the same time.

'What's that then?' Rosa smiled encouragingly.

'Well . . . we're doing a computing project together.' Gib cast a thumb in my direction, not taking his eyes off the tutor. 'And it has to be in by Monday and . . . we haven't finished it yet. And this is our last chance. If we don't finish it today then we'll lose thirty marks from our final assessment for the year.'

I stared at Gib, absolutely amazed. I shouldn't have been at all surprised, I know. I'd seen him in action often enough. He didn't fib all the time but when he was in trouble he was very, very good at it.

'So we were hoping that you'd let us use a PC at the back of the class maybe – if no one else is using it,' Gib finished.

'But I'm teaching a class.' Rosa frowned.

'Oh, we won't make a sound. Will we, Vicky?'

'Not a sound,' I agreed.

'I don't know about this . . .'

'Oh, please,' Gib pleaded. 'We won't make any noise. Honest. 'Cause otherwise we'll both fail computing this year.'

Rosa scrutinized us both so carefully that my face began to grow hot. Could you tell someone was lying just by looking at their face? I began to think you could.

'If you're both sure you'll not make any noise . . .' Rosa began.

'We won't,' Gib and I said eagerly.

97

'And you've got to leave when the class is over . . .'

'We will.'

'All right then,' Rosa said reluctantly. 'But mind – no noise now.' We shook our heads. 'You can use the table at the back with the two PCs on it.' Rosa pointed to the table.

Just then a man in a blue pinstripe suit and a woman in a white dress came into the room. They directed curious glances at us before they sat down.

Who wears a suit on a Saturday? I thought curiously.

'Come on then, Vicky,' Gib whispered. We sat down at the indicated table.

'Get cracking before we're found out,' Gib hissed in my ear.

'Help then,' I hissed back. 'Find out the name of the file that contains the dictionary for the spelling checker. That's important. Then make sure you can type it out.'

'Why do I have to do that?'

'I'll tell you in a minute.'

'You'll have to tell me what to do,' Gib replied.

Impatiently, I rummaged through my pockets to find something to write on. I found a piece of clean (I think!) but crumpled tissue and scribbled down the necessary commands. Gib gingerly picked up the tissue and laid it out flat before he started typing.

'I hope you haven't blown your nose on this!' he said with disdain.

I didn't bother to answer. I watched him type. Talk

about ponderous! I started typing myself. Connecting up to the live system was no problem. That was just a question of typing in the right data to Dad's connect program which was on the memory stick that I'd rescued from being taken by Eric. No, the problem would be logging on to an account on the live system when I didn't have a password.

Still, I had an idea about how to do that, but I needed to write a command file to do it for me. It wouldn't work with me typing directly from the PC. The bank's network system would suspect something strange was going on and disconnect itself from my PC if I tried to do it all manually rather than via a command file.

As we typed, two more men entered the room. Curious, they smiled at us. I smiled back. I carried on typing, peering intently at the screen as I did so. I wanted to make sure I got my command file absolutely right.

'I'm ready,' Gib said quietly after a few minutes.

I looked at his screen. He'd searched through the hard disc on the server which was set up for use by all the PCs in the school, just as I'd written down. There were a number of error messages until he found the right file. On the rest of his screen I saw:

> show helpdir: dictlarge
a
aardvark

99

```
aardvarks
aardwolf
aardwolves
aba
abaci
aback
abacus <break>
```

'Why did you want me to check the dictionary?' Gib whispered.

'I can't log on again using the TEST account 'cause that's only on the development system. And as the bank disabled Dad's account on the live system, I'm going to have to use another account.'

'Which one?'

'Eric, the Systems Manager's user account. It's the only account I can use where I know the privileges have been set up to do what I need to do on the bank's computer.'

'But you don't know the password,' Gib pointed out.

'This is the good bit,' I said softly. 'I've written a command file to make sure we log on to the live machine at Universal. It enters SYSTEM as the user name and then pulls out a word from the dictionary you found, to try as the password. If it doesn't work, the live computer will give out an error code which my file will read and then it will try the whole thing again with the next word down in the dictionary. And if my command

100

file works as it should, the bank's computer shouldn't lock me out after three false tries.'

Gib gave a low whistle. 'That's good! Will it work?'

'In theory. But I've never tried anything like this before,' I replied. 'And if Eric is anything like Dad and puts numbers in his passwords then it won't work. But according to Dad, no one follows the bank's rules and makes up unguessable passwords, because they all reckon they'll never be able to remember them. Dad's always trying to get all the bank staff to use passwords that aren't real words but very few people at the bank, if any, ever do.'

'So what do we do now?'

'We sit back and wait and hope that the password doesn't begin with a "z",' I explained.

I pressed the enter key on my keyboard to start my file running. Immediately, the dictionary was shown on Gib's PC and there the information began to scroll as each word was tried, just as I'd instructed in my command file.

'How long will it take if the password is right down at the other end of the alphabet?' Gib asked.

'Ages. Longer than we've got tonight. So keep your fingers crossed.'

Gib's frown was a reflection of my own.

'Is that really the fastest way of doing it?' he complained.

'Unless you already know a user name and password on the live system,' I stated.

'What happens if we haven't found the password by the time the class finishes?' Gib said. 'We've only got about an hour.'

'Then we'll just have to hang around the school and sneak back after everyone has gone,' I said jauntily.

I looked at Gib, my head high, hoping he'd tell me I was nuts and there was no way he was going to hang around until possibly midnight, waiting for a password that might not appear in the first place.

'All right then,' Gib said at last.

My heart sank to my ankles. I reckoned Mr Guy was more than likely to make sure that this classroom in particular was locked shut once evening classes were over. After all, he didn't want anyone running off with the school's expensive PCs.

What should we do? Allow ourselves to be locked in the room? Then how would we get out? Deciding to follow in Gib's footsteps, I decided we should wait to cross that bridge if and when we got to it. After all, we had every chance of getting a password that began with an 'A'.

'Stop looking on the pessimistic side,' I said to Gib.

Rosa had started her class by this time. The room was about half full, and she was talking about the World Wide Web and how it worked. I knew all that already but I saw that Gib was paying attention whilst trying not to look like he was. Rosa wittered on and the minutes ticked by slowly until I was off daydreaming in a world of my own. Then a sharp jab in the ribs woke me up.

'What d'you think you're playing at?' I said.

'Shush!' Gib looked around anxiously.

A few of the people towards the back of the class turned around to look at us.

'Oooops! Sorry!' I mouthed.

I turned to glare at Gib. He nodded towards my PC screen.

THE SYSTEM IS FOR THE EXCLUSIVE USE OF UNIVERSAL BANK PERSONNEL. ANY UNAUTHORIZED ACCESS TO THIS ACCOUNT MAY LEAD TO PROSECUTION. System>

I almost yelled out when I saw that. We were in! I double-checked this time to make sure I was on the live and not the development system.

'What's the last word to be read from your dictionary file?' I asked Gib, leaning across to read his screen.

'Cabbage?' Gib replied doubtfully.

'Cabbage! What a silly password!' I smiled. 'But remember that, Gib. We may need it again.'

Without wasting any more time, I tried to find the directory that contained the batch library file. In the end I did a global search over the whole system and I still couldn't find it.

'Maybe there isn't one?' Gib suggested, watching me closely.

'Well, I can't find it,' I said, angry at myself.

'What else do we need?'

'The transaction log file for the night the money was put into Dad's account,' I answered. 'I don't need the whole lot, just all the transactions over nine hundred thousand and under two million quid. I can always extend it later if I need to.'

'Go on then.'

This bit was easy. I'd seen Dad do it loads of times.

'What was Thursday's date?' I asked.

Gib considered. 'The 18th.'

SYSTEM>QUERY(*FROM TRANSACTIONS WHERE DATE= 18MAY AND AMT>900000 AND AMT<2000000

The data I wanted appeared almost immediately. Once I was happy it was what I wanted, I hit the <escape> key to stop the rest of the file being typed out. I then typed the same command again – but this time I asked for the results to be printed.

A message came up to tell me that the printout had started on printer 4. Our school had five high-speed printers kept in the small storage room next door to the classroom we were in. I knew I had to work fast. The chances of being discovered on the live system were even greater than being found on the development system, especially since I was using the Systems Manager's user account.

'Hang on a minute.' Gib frowned. 'That money was put into Dad's account in the early hours of yesterday morning.'

'So?'

'So yesterday was Friday, May the nineteenth, not the eighteenth.'

'Why didn't you say that before I started printing the file out?' I asked, annoyed.

It was too late to stop the printout. I typed in the command again, this time specifying: WHERE DATE=19MAY.

'I think I'll print out the files for the whole of this week, starting from Monday,' I said thoughtfully.

'Why do you want to do that?'

'It doesn't hurt to be thorough, and I might as well. We might find something interesting.'

'But it's just more paper to wade through,' Gib complained.

'Then I'll wade through it,' I retorted. 'You don't have to.'

'Keep your voice down. And I never said I wouldn't,' Gib said, 'though it'll probably be a complete waste of time.'

'It can't hurt though,' I argued.

I printed out the full transaction log files for Monday, Tuesday and Wednesday as well, praying that I'd get a chance to finish all this before the class came to a halt.

My screen messages showed that my printouts had finished printing just as Rosa was finishing off her lesson. Her class began to pack up and wander out.

'I'll have to log off now,' I whispered to Gib.

'Did you do everything you wanted to do?'

'Almost. I'll have to ask Dad about the batch library file on the live system. I don't understand why I couldn't find it,' I replied.

I logged off the bank's system. Gib and I switched off our PCs and stood up.

'Thank you very much,' I said to Rosa as we made our way out of the classroom.

'Yeah, thanks,' Gib added.

'Did you finish your homework?' Rosa asked.

'Oh yes, we did.' Gib said quickly. ' 'Bye.'

He grabbed my arm and almost pulled me out of the room.

We stopped off in the storage-room for our listings. Each listing ran to several pages. We gathered them up and scarpered.

When we got home, I let Gib take the listings to his room. He took both the printout from the development system which we'd done the previous night and the new printouts from the live system. I let him. I wanted to read them but I knew I was too tired to make much sense of them. I went to bed after cleaning my teeth and fell asleep immediately.

* ★ *

'Mum, do you want some help making lunch?' I offered after Sunday breakfast.

It was the strangest breakfast we'd ever had in our house. No one had anything to say. Dad ate in virtual silence, smiling at me very occasionally (smiles that didn't quite make it to his eyes), and Mum didn't say much at all. 'Do you want more bacon, Gib . . .? Pass the orange juice, Vicky . . .' But not a lot else.

And as for Gib. He could hardly keep his eyes open. At one point, his head nodded so far forward I thought his nose would end up in his beans for sure.

'We're not having lunch here today,' Mum replied. 'Beth and Sebastian have invited us all round to their house for lunch.'

'We're not going, are we?' I asked, dismayed.

'Yes, we are,' Mum said. 'I think we could all stand a change of scene.'

'Couldn't we go some other time?'

'No, we couldn't.' Mum frowned. 'Vicky, what's got into you this weekend?'

'Nothing.'

I thought of Dad and the maths test and the envelope in my jacket pocket that I still hadn't given to Mum and Dad.

'Hmm!' Mum said.

We set off for Aunt Beth and Sebastian's house at about one o'clock. Gib was just as reluctant to go as I

107

was – we wanted to go through the listings – except he'd had more sense than to say so out loud.

'Oh, I need to check something with you later,' Gib said softly from next to me in the back of the car.

'You two all right back there?' Dad asked.

'Fine, Dad.'

'Yeah, of course.'

'How are you feeling, dear?' Dad smiled at Mum.

Mum didn't return his smile. 'Tired,' she said, looking straight ahead.

Dad nodded. I looked out of the window.

We soon reached Aunt Beth's. She and Sebastian lived in a semi-detached house with three bedrooms, just a few miles away from us.

'Hi, everyone,' Aunt Beth said, smiling, the moment she opened the door. 'Come in, come in! I'd almost given up on you.'

Every time I went into their house I always noticed how quiet it was. And spotless. It was obvious they didn't have any children. Not a magazine, not a piece of paper, not a book was out of place. There was no dust or dirt or grime anywhere and every free centimetre of space was filled with a plant of some kind. It was like wading through an equatorial rain forest.

Sebastian emerged from their sitting room, a smile on his face. He rounded up Gib to show him a model of some airplane he had just finished working on.

We'd barely been in the house ten minutes when

Aunt Beth announced that lunch was ready. It was roast-lamb kebabs, rice and salad, followed by strawberries and vanilla ice-cream. One of the things I liked about Aunt Beth was that she could cook!

Gib and I didn't say much throughout lunch. Mum and Dad and Sebastian and Aunt Beth wittered on about boring grown-up things, the price of food, the price of clothes, the price of houses, the price of every-thing. I kept waiting for them to ask Dad what had happened in court yesterday – I wanted to know that bit myself – but nothing doing. I think it was another of those 'not in front of the children' jobs. Really annoy-ing! They talked about the forthcoming baby for a while which was a bit more interesting but nothing I hadn't already heard before.

'Babies are so expensive,' Aunt Beth said. Sebastian and Aunt Beth didn't have any children of their own so I wondered what they would know about it.

'I know,' Mum shrugged. 'But David and I have wanted another child for a long while. I just wish being pregnant didn't make me so tired all the time.'

'Have you got all the baby's things yet?' smiled Aunt Beth.

'Not yet.'

'You don't want to wait. The prices of prams and babies' clothes and toys go up pretty regularly.'

'It's a shame your salary at the bank doesn't go up as fast.' Sebastian smiled at Aunt Beth.

Aunt Beth smiled back, like there was no one else in the room with them. Sebastian reached out for Aunt Beth's hand. They were making goo-goo eyes at each other. Gib turned to me and pulled a face. I totally agreed! How wet could you get!

'If we're in the way just say so and we'll leave!' Dad teased.

Sebastian laughed and let go of Aunt Beth's hand. 'Sorry.'

'Don't forget, David,' Aunt Beth grinned, 'Sebastian is my second husband. We haven't been married as long as you two old fossils.'

'Fossil! I beg your pardon,' Mum said with mock indignation. 'Speak for yourself, Beth. You're older than me.'

'Thanks for reminding me,' Aunt Beth replied.

The grown-ups were off! I faded out for a few minutes, like turning down the volume on a television, until I heard Sebastian say, 'It'll get sorted out, David, just you wait and see.'

'I can't exactly do anything else.' Dad smiled slightly to take the sting out of his voice.

I looked at Gib. I'd missed what had brought this conversation up in the first place. I'd ask Gib later.

'I can't help thinking that it'd probably all be sorted out by now if they'd only run my weekend checking program,' Dad sighed. 'But Nicola, the General Manager, refuses to see past the nose on her face.'

'What do you mean, David?' Mum asked.

I wanted to know that too.

'My checking program runs on both the development and the live system. It reads through all the relevant program files on the development system and checks the transaction files on the live system for any strange anomalies,' Dad began. 'But Nicola reckons that I put a time trap in my program and that's how the million pounds got into my bank account in the first place, so she's ordered that none of my programs should be run until further notice.'

'What's a time trap, Dad?' I asked.

They all looked at me as if they'd forgotten Gib and I were at the table.

'It's a piece of code you write to only work on a certain day at a certain time,' Dad replied, before turning back to Sebastian and Aunt Beth. 'Now I reckon that if she'd just let my checking programs run on both systems, there'd be a report on all those things on the systems that need further investigation. And in one of those reports might have been a pointer to the person who really put the money in my account. Do you remember, Beth, how I caught you out a few weeks ago.'

Aunt Beth laughed. 'I sure do. I'd specified an end-of-month date incorrectly in one of my programs. I had input a date for last year instead of this year and the acceptance testers didn't spot the mistake.'

'But my program did,' Dad said stonily.

Aunt Beth nodded.

'Well, there's no point going on about it,' Dad sighed. 'If they didn't run it, they didn't run it. I'll just have to wait for my innocence to be proved another way.'

'And it will, David.' Mum smiled at Dad.

'It's a shame I'm on holiday for two weeks, David,' Aunt Beth frowned, 'otherwise I'm sure I could get Nicola to run your program. Mind you, as soon as I get back I'll ask her. I've already asked Eric to make sure that all the transaction logs and system changes are copied onto back-up media while I'm away, so that I can analyse them when I get back.'

'It's very good of you, Beth,' Dad said gratefully.

'Nonsense.'

'And if I can help in any way . . .' Sebastian left the rest unsaid.

I glanced at Gib and coughed, nodding towards the door. Gib frowned at me and carried on eating. The dimwit didn't get the hint at all. But I reckoned I was on to something.

Chapter Eight

Poking and Prying

I stood up.

Mum asked, 'Where are you going?'

'The loo!' I replied.

Mum and Dad exchanged a look and I walked to the door. I turned back to try and catch Gib's eye, but he was deeply involved with his roast lamb. I ran upstairs to the bathroom. Another good thing about Aunt Beth's house was that Gib and I could run everywhere and the sound would be muffled by their pile carpet so we never got bellowed at to 'Walk, don't run!' They had the same mid-grey carpet throughout the entire house and it looked really good.

Once in the bathroom, I locked the door and leaned against it. I knew why that money had been put in Dad's account. I was sure I was right. What had Dad said? Running his security program every Friday or Saturday was standard procedure? So the person who put that money in Dad's account must have done it to make sure that Dad's checking program didn't run. Whoever it was must have known that with Dad accused of taking all that money, no way would his programs be allowed to run on the computer. The question was, why the need to stop Dad's program from running in the first place? It must have been because the checking program would have revealed something. Something big. Something someone didn't want revealed.

But what?

And that still didn't tell me who was responsible for all this. But I was closer. I could feel it.

When Gib and I got home, we'd have to sit down and work through all those printouts we'd got from the bank's live system. If they didn't hold the answers then I'd just have to figure out what other files I should print out from the bank. The trouble was, each time I logged on to the bank's computer, I knew I stood a greater chance of getting caught. This was getting more and more dangerous.

I left the bathroom and was about to go downstairs again when I noticed one of the bedroom doors was slightly open. Being naturally interested in everything around me (in other words – nosy!), I tiptoed into the room. It was full of bookcases crammed with books. Books covered the floor in neatly stacked piles. Against one wall was a PC, exactly the same as the one Universal Bank had given Dad – before they took it away again.

The room was lovely. Just the sort of room I wanted

when I got my own house one day. I tiptoed out.

It's all right for some, I thought enviously.

Soon Gib or I would be sharing our room with a new brother or sister. And here Aunt Beth and Sebastian could devote one whole room to nothing but books. I tiptoed past the bathroom to the back room. It had a small double bed in it and a dressing table and that was it. Closing the door, I crept to the main bedroom at the front of the house. Wincing as the door handle made a noise as I turned it, I stepped inside.

Wow! Talk about luxury! Aunt Beth and Sebastian had the biggest bed I'd ever seen. Fitted wardrobes with mirrored fronts stood against one whole wall and a dressing table like something out of a magazine stood to the right of the window. I walked over to it. It was brilliant! Dark red-brown wood, with lots of drawers and covered with lotions and potions and bottles and jars. In the middle of the table was an open jewellery box, the prettiest I'd ever seen. Not that there was much jewellery inside. In fact, there was just a delicate gold bracelet. It looked like if you sneezed on it, it would disintegrate. Aunt Beth seemed to like that kind of very simple jewellery.

'Imagine having a box like this for just a pair of stud earrings, a necklace and a bracelet,' I muttered to myself.

What a waste!

But then I caught sight of a slip of paper just sticking up from under the empty ring tray. I took a quick glance around before lifting up the tray and taking out the piece of paper. It was two pieces of paper actually. Two airline tickets to be precise. I opened the top one.

Destination: Rio de Janeiro via Air France. And the date on the ticket was for three days' time – Wednesday.

Talk about being doubly all right for some! I flicked through both tickets then put them back and replaced the ring tray on top of them.

Then I caught sight of Aunt Beth's perfume.

Chanel Number 19. Mum's favourite. Only Mum wouldn't even let me breathe near her bottle. I stretched out my hand towards it.

'Vicky, what are you doing?'

My head whipped around at the sound of Sebastian's voice.

'I . . . er . . . I . . .'

'Vicky? Victoria Gibson, what on earth are you doing in there? Couldn't you find the bathroom?' Mum appeared behind Sebastian and she looked seriously annoyed.

'I wasn't doing anything,' I said quickly, my face on fire.

'No harm done,' Sebastian said lightly.

'I . . . I just wanted to look around your house . . . 'cause it's so pretty.' My excuse was lame – even to my ears. But it was the truth.

'Vicky, you should know better,' Mum said, one hand

116

on her hip. 'You had no business going where you hadn't been invited.'

'I didn't do any harm,' I protested.

'That's not the point and you know it,' Mum said.

'What's going on here?'

Dad, Gib and Aunt Beth had turned up now. I was desperately praying for the carpet to move aside to reveal a large hole that would swallow me up.

'I wasn't doing any harm, Dad, I promise,' I said quickly as he opened his mouth to speak.

'Victoria, what are you doing in here?' Dad frowned. 'I thought you said . . .'

'It's no big deal,' Aunt Beth soothed. 'If Sebastian and I don't mind then why should anyone else? You were just looking around, Vicky, weren't you?'

I nodded.

Sebastian's eyes were laughing. He ran a hand over his wavy blond hair.

'Dad, I didn't take anything, honest I didn't,' I pleaded.

'No one said you did,' Dad replied firmly.

'I just like their house. It's so neat. I've never seen a house so neat and tidy . . .' I couldn't think of anything else to say so I shut up.

'Come out of there, Victoria,' Dad beckoned to me.

I walked out of the room, my head bent, and Sebastian closed the door behind me.

Once downstairs, the subject got on to holidays. Aunt Beth and Sebastian talked about their forthcoming visit to Rio.

'We're only going for seven days. It's all we could afford,' Aunt Beth sighed.

'But what a seven days, eh!' Sebastian raised his eyebrows a few times in Aunt Beth's direction.

We stayed for about another hour until Mum said she was getting tired. At last it was time to leave. I hadn't said a single word since being found in Sebastian and Aunt Beth's bedroom. I'd sat on the sofa, examining my shoes, the entire time. I wanted to crawl away and *die*. I'd never, ever been so embarrassed. I couldn't leave their house fast enough. Gib kept giving me funny-peculiar looks. I swore if he started laughing I'd punch his face in!

'Vicky,' Mum said, once we reached home. 'The next time you're thinking about being nosy – don't!'

'I wasn't . . .' I began, but I couldn't finish – because I was!

'Right, you two. Off to your rooms to do your homework,' Dad said.

'Hang on. Dad, can I ask you a question?' I said.

'A homework question?' Dad asked.

'A bank question,' I replied.

'Vicky, I don't think . . .' Mum began.

'It's all right, Laura. Let her ask,' interrupted Dad.

'You said that at Universal, the development system

118

and the live system are exactly the same,' I began, choosing my words carefully.

'Yes. So?'

'So why isn't the batch library file in the same directory on the live system as it is on the development system?' I asked.

Dad shrugged. 'Because you don't need it on the live system. Only the linked files – the finished programs – get copied across to the live system, so you don't need information on that system about when the object files were created and when each program was first written and suchlike. We just make sure the two systems are the same when it comes to running the programs.'

'Oh, I see. Is it the people who test the programs who put the information about each program into the batch library file?' I asked.

'No, the acceptance testers don't do that. There's a program which automatically picks up the dates and times from all the other programs and adds their details to the batch library,' Dad explained.

'So what do the acceptance testers do – exactly?'

'Vicky . . .' Mum said warningly.

'It's all right. I'm glad she's interested.' Dad smiled. 'Once a programmer is happy that his or her program is working, they give the source code to someone in the acceptance testing team who then checks the code, compiles it and links it and tests the running program on the development system. If that all works then the final version – the linked file – gets copied across on to the live system,' Dad said. 'Why all the questions?'

'Just interested,' I bluffed. 'Mum, please can I borrow your laptop?' I asked, trying to change the subject.

'Oh yeah!' Gib breathed.

I glared at him. What a moron! What was he trying to do – give me away?

'What d'you want it for?' Mum asked.

'Part of my homework,' I replied, crossing my fingers behind my back. 'You can have it back in about an hour.'

'No, I don't need it tonight. You can take it.' Mum shrugged. 'Just bring it back downstairs tomorrow.'

'OK, Mum. Thanks.' Mum's laptop was ancient with a prehistoric version of the operating system. She had word processing and spreadsheet software on it and that was it. But it'd be enough.

'Wait a minute, Victoria,' Dad frowned. 'How did you know there's no batch file on the live system?'

That was the one question I was hoping Dad wouldn't ask.

'Er . . . from what you and Aunt Beth said earlier,' I replied, mentally crossing my fingers.

'I think I *will* go and do my homework now,' Gib said quickly.

Dad's frown deepened. He put his hand on Gib's forehead. 'What? No arguments? No complaints? What's the matter, Gib? Are you ill?'

And just like that, Gib got me off the hook. I could have kissed him!

'Get off, Dad!' Gib said, pulling away. 'I do my homework sometimes you know.'

'Not according to your school report,' Mum said. 'Gib, I wish you could be more like your sister.'

I caught Gib's bitter grimace before he turned away from me.

'You shouldn't say that, Mum. Gib doesn't like it,' I said quietly. 'You shouldn't keep comparing his schoolwork to mine. You shouldn't keep saying he should be more like me.'

Surprised, Mum looked at me and Gib. I looked down at the carpet. Gib looked across to the opposite wall. I felt rather than saw Mum and Dad exchanging a glance.

'Sorry,' Mum said seriously. 'I'll stop comparing.'

I picked up the laptop from behind the armchair and left the room. Gib was behind me. We ran upstairs.

'Walk! Don't run!' Dad yelled.

'In here.' Gib pointed to his room, once we got to the landing. He barged in front of me. I followed him, shutting his bedroom door behind me. Stepping on the few remaining bits of exposed carpet, I picked my way through the comics and clothes strewn all over the floor, trying to make my way to Gib's one bedroom chair.

'Right then,' Gib said. 'First of all, what were you doing in Aunt Beth's room earlier?'

'Mind your own,' I snapped.

'Which is obviously what you *weren't* doing?' Gib's tone was really snide.

I tapped my nose but said nothing. Gib flopped down on to the floor.

'What about that letter from Miss Hiff? Are you really going to give it to Dad and Mum?' Gib asked.

'I haven't got much choice,' I sighed. 'I'm just waiting for the right moment.'

'Rather you than me,' Gib said drily.

'Never mind that. What about the listings we got yesterday?'

'I spent half the night going through those,' Gib said. 'I couldn't see anything. But then I wasn't too sure what I was supposed to be looking for.'

'Let's have a look,' I said.

I cleared some space on the floor – which took ages – and lay down on my stomach, going through the first listing Gib gave me. It was the transaction log file for the early hours of Friday morning. It was later on that same day when the million pounds was found in Dad's account.

'You can check through Friday's and Thursday's listings and I'll do the beginning of the week again,' Gib said.

'OK,' I replied.

And we started reading.

Two hours later, my neck ached, my eyes ached, my

back ached, even my blood ached. Gib and I had swapped listings to check each other's checking, and although I still had one more listing to check, as yet neither of us had found anything useful. Friday's transaction log had a line which stated that the money had indeed been put in David P. Gibson's bank account, but there was nothing about which cashier had entered the details and which cashier had verified the details, the way there was for every other transaction in the file. The lack of cashier information was the bank's so-called proof that the money was transferred using Dad's checking program. After all, they reasoned, no one would write a program to put money in someone else's account.

I rolled over onto my back and stretched out.

'Every muscle in my body is hurting,' I complained.

'Shall I get us something to eat and drink?' Gib volunteered.

'If you're offering,' I said, surprised.

Gib stood up, shook out his legs and off he went. He came back ten minutes later with two scrubby sandwiches he'd made, a packet of chocolate biscuits and two glasses of apple juice. Not a bad effort, I thought.

Without a word we carried on reading through our listings. I checked, double-checked and triple-checked each line on each page until my eyes felt like they were only being held in my head by a single thread. I had the beginnings of a really bad headache and I still hadn't found anything.

'Wait a minute . . .' Gib said slowly.

'What? What is it? Have you found something?' I asked eagerly, shuffling across the floor to where Gib lay, surrounded by listing paper.

Gib looked at me. 'Let me check something first.'

Impatiently I waited as he flicked through sheets of listings.

'Well? What is it?' I asked again.

'I was just looking at this batch library file we got from the development system.'

'Why are you doing that? It's a total waste of time. We should be checking the printouts from the live system.'

'Do you want to hear this or not?' Gib snapped. He can be a real toad sometimes!

'I'm listening,' I replied.

'You remember when we were going through this in the garden? You said the first column gives you the name of the program, the second column shows when the program was first created, the third column shows when the object file was created, which means when the program was compiled or translated, and the fourth column shows when the program was linked with all the other programs. Is that right?' Gib asked slowly.

I nodded.

'Look at this.' Gib pointed to a page in the middle of the printout directly in front of him.

```
TIMESTAT03jan:1335.05mar:1317.05 mar:1503.
   sjones        12000
TIMESLDD12jan:0650.12apr:0816.apr:1934.
   vamritraj    58702
TIMESLP01feb:1149.02feb:1659.02feb:1705.
   jkennedy     4250
TIMETRV30mar:0149.16may:2012.15may:2149.
   ejones        8500
TIMETZG28jan:0821.28mar:1037.28mar:1252.
   jkennedy     76000
```

'What exactly am I supposed to be looking at?' I asked as each line began to merge with the others as I read.

'Look at that program TIMETRV,' Gib ordered.

I looked at him. He was ready to burst. His eyes were on fire as he watched me. I turned back to the listing with a frown and read the TIMETRV line again.

'I don't see anything.'

After all the time I'd spent goggle-eyed going through the listings, I wouldn't have seen Mount Everest if it was perched at the end of my nose.

'Look at when TIMETRV was linked.'

I read the listing. 'May the fifteenth, at eleven minutes to ten. So?'

'Now look at when the object file was created.' Gib's eyes gleamed.

'May the sixteenth, twelve minutes past . . .'

Then I got it.

'You see! You see!' Gib sat up quickly. 'You said you have to compile the code first which produces an object file and then you link the object file.'

'That's right,' I nodded, the blood rushing in my ears. 'In which case . . .'

'How could the object file be created a whole day *after* the linked file was created?' Gib said.

'That's not possible,' I mused.

'But there it is.' Gib pointed to the line again.

'TIMETRV . . . I wonder what that program does?'

'Dad will know,' Gib pointed out.

'Do you think anyone else has noticed this?' I asked.

Gib shrugged. 'I haven't a clue. But I bet everyone's looking on the live system and no one's paying much attention to the development system. Why should they?'

'But you can't transfer money from the development computer, so why fiddle about with the programs on that system?' I asked.

'That's what we have to find out,' Gib replied.

I stood up. 'I think we're definitely on to something.' My voice was shaking.

'There's another thing,' Gib grinned.

'What's that?' I asked, all ears.

'Take a look at the programmer's name! It's *ejones!*' Gib said smugly. 'Eric Jones, the Systems Manager.'

I stared at Gib. I couldn't believe it. Eric . . . Eric had put all that money in Dad's account . . . Of course! It all

126

made sense. And being the System Manager, Eric was in the ideal position to fiddle the system.

'What are we going to do?' I asked. 'Should we tell Dad?'

'What do you think? Should we? Is the batch library listing enough proof?' Gib asked.

I shook my head slowly. 'I doubt it. Eric's probably got a perfectly reasonable explanation for it. We have to find out what it means, or even if it means anything at all. It could mean nothing. We can't afford to give ourselves away and warn Eric that we're on to him. We must check it out first and if it does mean something, then we'll tell Dad what we've found.'

Gib and I ran downstairs to the living room, leaving the listings upstairs.

'When will you children learn to walk and not thunder down those stairs?' Dad sighed as we entered the room.

'Dad, does Eric at the bank write programs that get tested by the acceptance testers and put in the batch library file?' Gib asked.

I licked my lips. My heart was hammering. So close . . .

'Of course he doesn't!' Dad laughed. 'Eric's not a programmer. He's in charge of the operators and the computers.'

'But he *could* write programs if he wanted to?' I asked eagerly.

'No, he couldn't.' Dad frowned. 'He doesn't know how to. Besides, why would he want to?'

'Are you sure?' I asked.

Dad nodded. 'What are you two up to?' he asked suspiciously. 'Why all the questions about Eric all of a sudden?'

'No reason in particular,' Gib replied quickly.

'How can you be so sure, Dad?' I persisted. 'Eric might write programs . . .'

'Eric hates programming. He thinks it's the most boring part of computing.' Dad shook his head. 'He always says he'd rather beat himself over the head with a metal tray than write a program. Now what's all this about?'

'Vicky and I are doing a project for school,' Gib replied immediately. 'What does the TIMETRV program do?'

'Gib, don't you start.'

I could see Mum was getting annoyed now.

'I wish I knew what you two are up to.' Dad's eyes narrowed as he watched each of us in turn. 'If you must know, the TIMETRV program is part of the transaction log report program – if memory serves. It uses the computer system clock to time-stamp all the entries in the log file.'

'So it doesn't transfer money or anything like that?' Gib asked.

Dad shook his head. 'No. It's just a noddy program

that runs each night when the transaction log file is created. And just where did you two learn about the TIMETRV program?'

'Aunt Beth must've mentioned it,' I said, crossing my fingers behind my back.

'Now, that's enough.' Mum stood up. 'Even if your father isn't getting upset, I am.'

'Sorry, Dad, sorry, Mum,' Gib said quickly. 'Come on, Vicky.' We went out into the hall and ran upstairs.

'WALK! I give up!' I heard Dad exclaim.

In Gib's room I turned to him. Gib beamed at me.

'We're finally on the right track,' he said happily. 'I just know we are.'

'But Dad said that Eric . . .'

'That doesn't mean anything,' Gib interrupted. 'I'll bet you anything that Eric *does* know how to write programs. I bet he's an ace programmer. I think we should tell Dad. Then he can tell the bank and the police and they can arrest Eric and . . .'

'Whoa, Sherlock!' I pursed my lips. 'Now tell me how we *prove* it. That money was put in Dad's account, not Eric's – remember?'

'But it says *ejones* in the batch library file,' Gib frowned.

'So what? Eric could have a perfectly good explanation for that and, even if he doesn't, the bank and the police will say that Dad could've put *ejones* in the file himself to throw everyone off the scent. We need proof that Eric put that money in Dad's account and we need to know *why*.'

'Hmm!' Gib's smile faded.

He sat down on the floor. I sat opposite. Our heads on our hands, we both had a long, hard think.

Chapter Nine

A Slip of the Tongue

The next morning a dull-grey, cloudy sky threatened rain. Chaucy arrived at our house around a quarter to eight to walk to school with Gib. I had the misfortune to be the one who opened the door for him. Immediately, he started grinning at me. His constant grin was really cheesing me off. I glared at him. 'I'm glad you can find something funny in all this.' I had the satisfaction of seeing the smile slip off his face.

'Victoria, I wasn't laughing . . .'

Ignoring him, I went back into the kitchen to finish my breakfast.

'Gib's upstairs in his room,' I said when Chaucy followed me into the kitchen.

Chaucy danced uncomfortably from foot to foot as he watched me.

'I wasn't laughing because I think what you and Gib are going through is funny,' Chaucy said.

Then what were you grinning like an idiot about? I

thought frostily, spooning cornflakes into my mouth. I thought if I ignored him, he'd bug off.

'You don't . . . like me much, do you?' Chaucy said quietly.

Surprised, I turned to face him. 'Like you? I . . . well, I . . .'

'Why not?' Chaucy asked.

I'd never seen him looking so serious. My face fell as I watched him. All of a sudden I felt really uncomfortable. Really nasty. I began to squirm on my chair.

'You don't like me much either,' I defended myself.

'Yes I do,' Chaucy replied immediately.

It was just as well I was sitting down when he said that or I would have keeled over from shock. My whole body went hot – even my fingernails.

'You do?' I whispered.

Chaucy nodded.

For a brief second I believed him. Until I remembered all the times Chaucy and Gib had stood side by side, laughing at me. He was probably on a serious wind-up now. This whole act was probably something he'd set up with Gib.

'You don't fool me, Alexander Chaucer. I know you're just pulling my leg,' I said with disgust.

'I'm not,' Chaucy protested.

'All right then. If you like me so much, why are you always laughing at me? You're always making me feel really stupid.' I glared at him to let him know that I

132

knew what he was up to. This was a wind-up if ever I saw one.

'I never laugh at you.' If the shock in Chaucy's voice was put on then he deserved an Oscar.

I sat back in my chair. 'I'm not daft you know,' I said angrily. 'I have eyes. I only have to look at you before you start grinning. Do I really look that funny?'

'I'm *smiling* at you. I've been trying to show you I like you for ages,' Chaucy said. His face was a deep shade of beetroot now.

I stared at him. Even his neck had turned fiery red. I didn't know what to say. He looked so embarrassed that I knew he was serious. I got even more angry with him.

'Take a tip from me then,' I offered. 'Don't grin at me. Your smile is *not* your best feature.'

'I'll remember that,' Chaucy smiled, then quickly stopped. For the first time he looked almost sane. Only then did it sink in. Chaucy *liked* me. An embarrassed silence fell between us.

'I . . . I . . . er . . . I'll go and find Gib,' Chaucy stammered, and he tore out of the kitchen as if he'd been shot from a cannon.

I couldn't get over it. *He liked me.* But he was still a prize twit!

Ten minutes later, I was up in my room, writing out a fresh envelope for Miss Hiff's letter that I'd brought home. Mum was having a late lie-in and Dad was downstairs watching telly after helping Gib and me prepare our breakfast. Dad was in a very sombre mood. He tried to pretend that the break from work was just what he needed, but anyone with half an eye could see he was missing it. Now was obviously not the best time to hand over Miss Hiff's letter. Yesterday evening, I had waited for the ideal moment to arrive, so that I could explain what had happened at school. I'd waited . . . and waited. Deep down, I knew that there would never be an ideal moment. If it carried on like this, I'd never hand over the letter and then Mum and Dad would hear all about it from Miss Hiff instead of me. And I certainly didn't want that. I couldn't risk Miss Hiff trying to phone Dad at home, or worse still, at work. She wouldn't do anything today though (fingers crossed!). I reckoned she'd wait all day to hear from Dad. So I had one more day, at the very most. Tonight. I'd do it tonight. Not now though. The thought of it had my heart pounding.

Looking down at the envelope, I sighed and wondered what Gib and Chaucy were doing. If Chaucy *had* been winding me up after all then I'd never speak to him again! Never, never!

There was a knock at my door. It had to be Mum or Dad. Gib had never knocked in his life. Hiding the envelope under my pillow, I said, 'Come in.'

It was Chaucy, closely followed by Gib who closed the door behind him.

'What do you two want?' I frowned, ready to laugh back if I was laughed at first.

'I told Chaucy about what we did yesterday,' Gib said.

'I want to help,' added Chaucy.

I wondered if there was anything Gib *wouldn't* tell his best friend?

'What can you do?' I asked Chaucy.

'I don't know. I just wanted you to know that I can help if you need it,' Chaucy said.

I shrugged. 'OK.'

'Are you coming to school now?' Gib asked.

'No, I've got something to finish,' I replied, holding up the envelope.

'What's that?' Chaucy asked.

I tapped my nose. 'See you at school,' I said and turned back to my envelope.

I was walking with Gayle and Maggie on our way to the canteen for lunch when Miss Hiff passed us in the corridor. I lowered my head and walked faster, but it was no use.

'Ah, Vicky, I was looking for you,' Miss Hiff said from behind me.

Grimacing, I stopped in my tracks and turned slowly.

'Hello, Miss Hiff,' I said faintly.

Miss Hiff nodded at me. 'When can I expect a call from your father?'

'Er . . . some time today, miss, I w-would think,' I said.

'I hope so.' Miss Hiff frowned. 'Otherwise I shall be phoning him at work first thing tomorrow morning.'

'No, Miss Hiff,' I panicked. 'He'll phone you. He said he would.' The last thing I wanted was for Miss Hiff to find out that Dad had been suspended from his bank. The headmistress eyed me suspiciously.

'Tomorrow, Victoria,' she said at last.

'Yes, miss.'

I dug my hands deep into my jacket pockets, terrified that Miss Hiff would see the letter with a brand-new envelope in my right-hand pocket. I'd wanted to leave it at home, but what if Mum or Dad found it? Bringing it to school made me break out in an ice-cold sweat every time I walked past a teacher, but so far so good. I'd never done anything like this before – and never again!

I'd dug a hole for myself by reading the letter and I could see no way out of it. Miss Hiff drew herself up to her full one metre nothing and marched on.

'What was that all about?' Maggie asked curiously.

I sighed, then shrugged. 'The maths exam last Friday,' I said, plumping for the truth.

Goodness! That was only three days ago. Such a lot had happened since then. I felt like I was spinning and spinning and I couldn't stop. Everything was happening at once and I couldn't control it.

'Yeah, I meant to ask you what all that was about. Did you cheat?' Gayle asked.

Shocked, I stopped walking and looked at her. I was dangerously close to forgetting that Gayle was one of my best friends.

'What do you think?' I asked angrily.

'I would say not, but you never know . . .' Gayle trailed off as she looked at Maggie.

Maggie glanced down at her shoes, a slow flush creeping over her face. I frowned at both of them. Then I remembered Maggie with her nose deep in her pencil-case during our maths exam. If I'd seen her then maybe Gayle had too.

'Anyway, they don't think I was cheating *in* the exam,' I explained. 'Someone stole the answers beforehand and they think it was me 'cause I finished so quickly.'

'Whereas we all know it was the Hacker Supreme.' Maggie grinned.

'So *that's* what the fuss was all about,' Gayle breathed. 'Someone actually fleeced the answers?'

'Yeah, only I didn't do it,' I said fiercely. 'The trouble is . . .' Just then someone tapped me on the shoulder. It was Gib.

'Where are you going?' he asked, ignoring my friends.

'For some lunch,' I replied. Since when was Gib interested in my eating habits?

'We can use a PC in the science block,' Gib said pointedly.

'For what?'

'The *ejones* proof,' he replied.

I understood at once.

'Gayle, Maggie, I'll catch up with you later,' I told them.

'Vicky . . .' Gayle protested. 'It's jam tart for afters.'

'I've got something important to do,' I said quickly. 'Honest.'

'Oh, all right then,' Gayle said, in a voice that said it wasn't all right.

I left them to it and walked with Gib to the science block.

'Chaucy's holding a PC for us,' Gib explained, 'so we can try to get the proof we need that Eric put that money in Dad's account.'

'How do we do that?'

'I haven't a clue. I was hoping you'd know that,' Gib replied.

Typical!

'Look, now isn't a very good time to hack into the bank's system,' I said. 'I'm far more likely to be discovered by one of their operators if I use it now.'

'We can't use the computers here tonight. The evening computer courses go on all week and we can't use the same excuse twice. That tutor, Rosa, is bound to ask us more questions this time,' Gib pointed out.

'I suppose so . . .' I conceded.

I stopped in my tracks and stared at Gib. It was as if a light bulb had just been switched on in my head.

'Gib, I've got to do something,' I told him.

'What?' he frowned.

'Something,' I said impatiently. 'Are you going to be in Room Twenty-two or Twenty-four?'

'Room Twenty-two,' Gib frowned.

I started to run back to the canteen.

'But Vicky . . .'

'I'll see you in a few minutes,' I called out to him.

I raced to the canteen. One single thought kept hammering in my head and I couldn't get it to go away. There was something I had to find out. I caught up with Maggie and Gayle, who'd been joined by Carolyn, just as they were sitting down with their lunch trays.

'Maggie, can I talk to you?' I puffed.

'Go on then,' she said, surprised.

'Outside,' I said.

She frowned at me.

'It's important. I'll be quick,' I told her.

Slowly, Maggie stood up and I followed her out of the canteen to stand just outside the door. I waited until a group of five from another class walked past us into the canteen before speaking.

'Maggie, how . . . how did you know the name of the person who stole Mrs Bracken's maths answers?' I asked.

'What're you talking about?' Maggie frowned.

'You heard me,' I said carefully. 'How did you know the person's name?'

'I didn't. I don't. Unless you told me just now.' Maggie shrugged.

'I didn't say one word about the person's name,' I said.

'I don't know what you're talking about.'

'I'm talking about the "Hacker Supreme",' I said coldly. 'That's the first thing you said when I told you why I was hauled up in front of Miss Hiff.'

'It's just an expression. I didn't mean anything by it,' Maggie scowled. She tried to walk past me back into the canteen. I pushed the door shut to stop her.

'Oh no you don't,' I said. '*You're* the person who pinched the exam answers.'

'Don't be ridiculous,' Maggie said furiously.

'I'm not. There's no way you could know what the real culprit signed at the bottom of the message left for Crackly Bracken unless you're that person.'

'Listen, I know nothing about someone breaking into Mrs Bracken's PC and leaving messages,' Maggie said, her eyes narrowed.

I folded my arms across my chest. 'How did you know the real thief broke into Mrs Bracken's PC? I never said that. I said the exam answers had been pinched.'

Maggie's mouth dropped open. 'You said something about a hacker . . .'

'No. *You* said it, I didn't. It *was* you,' I said.

'Go to hell.'

'No I won't!' I hissed. 'You got me into dead serious trouble. Miss Hiff is talking about suspending me for hacking into Mrs Bracken's file, and it wasn't me – it was you.'

'You reckon all this just because I said Hacker Supreme?' Maggie said scornfully.

'That and the fact that you knew about the message being on Crackly Bracken's PC. I didn't mention that bit just now.'

'Move, Vicky,' Maggie ordered. 'My lunch is getting cold.'

'It's going to get a lot colder,' I told her. 'I want you to tell Miss Hiff that it was you and not me who pinched the answers to the maths exam.'

'I'll do no such thing,' Maggie said indignantly.

'If you don't, I will. I'm not a snitch but I'm not going to get suspended for you. No way,' I fumed.

Maggie's fists clenched at her sides. My body went stiff. I dropped my arms, ready for her.

'I thought you were my friend,' Maggie said.

'I am. But if you were *my* friend you wouldn't let me take the blame for you,' I replied. 'I'm going to see Miss Hiff. Right this minute.' I turned to march away from her. Maggie grabbed me by my arm – hard.

'Vicky, you can't. Not that I'm admitting for a moment that I did it,' Maggie added quickly.

'Then why grab my arm?' I asked frostily. 'We'll just see what Miss Hiff has to say about all this.'

'Vicky, please. You . . . you don't understand.' Maggie was close to tears now. 'My dad's just started his own business and I have to type all his letters and invoices because he can't afford a proper, full-time secretary. I haven't had time to do my homework or revise or anything. Mum and Dad have been arguing about it for months. If I say anything, Miss Hiff will call my parents up to the school and then things will just get worse.'

Maggie looked absolutely miserable. I didn't know what to do.

'Why don't you tell your dad that you can't do his work and your own as well?' I suggested.

'What? And give Dad and Mum more to quarrel about? Things are bad enough at home as it is,' Maggie replied. Her eyes were shimmering, her lips turned down.

'Maggie, I'm sorry. I really am. But I'm not going to let myself get excluded from school for you or anyone else.'

I felt like a right cow saying that, but what choice did I have?

'Please, Vicky. I'll make it up to you. I swear I will,' Maggie pleaded.

'No, Maggie. I'm sorry but I can't.' I shook my head. 'Why on earth did you leave that message at the bottom of Crackly Bracken's file anyway? It was a stupid thing to do.'

'It . . . I was just showing off, I suppose,' Maggie said unhappily. 'It seemed like a funny thing to do at the time.'

'Well, it wasn't, it was stupid,' I replied. 'You should never have done it. You should never have cheated.'

'Vicky, please . . .'

'No, Maggie,' I said firmly.

'If you tell on me, I swear I'll never speak to you again. And what's more, I'll make sure that everyone knows what a grass you are. No one will speak to you,' Maggie threatened.

She shouldn't have said that. I'd been feeling really bad up until then and wondering if maybe there wasn't a way to keep Maggie out of it and get away with it myself. But when she said that . . .

'Go ahead – if you think you're bad,' I replied.

Maggie drew herself up and gave me the filthiest look she could. She took her time over it too.

'Get out of my way,' she said, pushing me.

'Fight! Fight!' someone called out from inside the canteen. Looking at Maggie, I knew she wanted me to push her back. She wanted to fight. I was really tempted to push her back. I was just in the mood for a fight myself. But I didn't. She pushed me again, before walking past me back into the canteen. I watched her as she walked towards her table. I saw her point at me as she started to speak to Gayle and Carolyn. I turned around and went to the girls' loos. I put the toilet lid down and sat.

'You had no choice, Victoria,' I tried to tell myself.

It didn't help. Now I wished I had pushed her back. Inside, I was raging angry – at everything and everyone. All the anger and the hurt sat inside my chest like a concrete football. Burying my head in my hands, I wished myself away on another planet in another galaxy. I just wanted to be as far away from school and home as possible.

I mean, what did Maggie expect? How could she possibly make it up to me? Detention was one thing, getting excluded was something else entirely. Over and over, I kept going through my reasons for not taking the blame. Each one was valid, reasonable. So why didn't they make me feel better? Maggie had been my friend since we were in Infants together.

What was I going to do? If I told on Maggie, I knew she meant it. She'd never speak to me again.

Chapter Ten

Please Yourself

'What happened to you this lunchtime? Chaucy and I sat like lemons waiting for you.'

Gib barged into my room after the barest knock. I'd been avoiding him all afternoon at school. I'd been avoiding everyone, but I knew he'd catch up with me eventually.

'Sorry,' I muttered. 'Something else came up.'

'Something more important than proving Dad innocent?' Gib exploded.

I didn't answer.

'You don't give a monkey's what happens to Dad, do you? All you care about is yourself.'

'That's not true – or fair.' I leaped out of my chair. 'Something else came up that I had to deal with, that's all.'

'And meanwhile, Eric's in the clear and Dad might go to prison. I got Eric's phone number from the staff file we printed out and phoned his house. His wife said he was at work so he hasn't skipped off to the Bahamas yet, but for all we know he might be planning to leave at any second,' Gib fumed.

'Talk sense, Gib,' I snapped. 'What would he use for money? That million was found in Dad's account not his, and the bank hasn't reported any more money missing . . .'

'That doesn't mean that Eric isn't up to something. Dad still needs our help. If you keep dossing about, Eric will get away,' Gib said furiously.

'Then why don't *you* stop him? Why leave everything to me?' I snapped back.

'If I knew how to use the computer to get the proof Dad needs then I wouldn't bother you,' Gib said. 'But I don't. And Chaucy might be good at computing but he doesn't know the Universal Bank system.'

'I said I was sorry,' I sighed. 'Besides, I think I've worked out how it was done . . .'

'But what if it's too late?'

I tried hard to hold on to my temper. I gritted my teeth and said, 'Gib, do you want to know my idea or not? You said yourself that Eric is at work, pretending everything is as normal. He has no idea we're on to him.'

Gib glared at me. 'I guess I can't expect anything different from you. After all . . .'

My bedroom went deathly quiet.

'After all – what? Go on. Finish what you were going to say,' I prompted.

'I was going to say, after all you are only a girl,' Gib finished.

'Yeah, I bet you were,' I scoffed.

'Yes I was,' Gib replied vehemently.

'Well, now that you've said it, get lost!' I barked at him. 'I've got things to do.'

Gib left the room, slamming my bedroom door shut behind him. I stared at the closed door. What was happening? I'd had more quarrels in the last few days than I'd had in my entire life. And I hated it.

'Can I get you anything, Mum? A cup of tea? Coffee? Do you want anything, Dad?'

Mum and Dad exchanged a rueful glance before they both turned to look at me.

'No thank you, pumpkin,' Dad smiled.

It was seven o'clock and we'd just finished dinner. I'd helped Dad cook it and I'd loaded up the dishwasher all by myself, without being asked. I'd even volunteered to mop the kitchen floor afterwards.

This was it! Time to give Dad and Mum the letter from Miss Hiff. I couldn't put it off any longer, but I had to choose my moment.

'How are you feeling, Dad?' I asked.

'I think I'll go and do my homework.' Gib stood up quickly and scarpered. Coward!

'I feel fine, Victoria.' Dad raised his eyebrows but said nothing else.

'Mum, why don't you have a lie down? You should rest,' I told her.

'I am resting,' Mum replied.

Mum and Dad exchanged another look. I wondered if I was overdoing it. I licked my lips nervously.

'Come on, Victoria – out with it!' Dad laughed. 'The suspense is killing me.'

'Out with what?' I asked, playing innocent.

'Vicky, we might have been born yesterday but it was early in the morning,' Mum told me with a smile. 'What's the matter?'

Desperately, I tried to think of some suitable answer. Nothing came to mind, so I decided on the truth.

'You're not supposed to get upset, Mum,' I muttered.

'Oh dear! Is it that bad?' Mum sighed.

I nodded slowly.

'Then I'll stay sitting down,' Mum said. 'Now, what is it?'

Reluctantly, I dug into the pocket of my jeans and got out Miss Hiff's now severely crumpled letter. I gave it to Dad, who took it gingerly between his thumb and finger. Looking at it again, I had to admit that it did look rather manky. I watched as Dad opened the envelope.

'I'll put the envelope in the bin for you if you like,' I offered eagerly, practically snatching the envelope out of his hands.

Dad put the letter between him and Mum and they both started reading. I had to force myself to walk, not run from the room. But I walked really quickly. Once I was in the kitchen, I tore the envelope into tiny pieces and dropped them in the wastebin. At least the problem of the envelope was out of the way. Then I legged it out of the kitchen and up the stairs – or at least, I tried.

'Victoria! Get down here!' Dad hollered before I'd even got halfway.

I was tempted to pretend I hadn't heard him.

'VICTORIA! NOW!' Dad yelled.

I turned around and walked back down, dragging my feet. My heart was pounding like a pneumatic drill and tears welled up in my eyes. I suddenly felt so cold. I wondered if I should give in and cry and get Dad and Mum's sympathy up front? In spite of how slowly I was walking, I reached the living room.

'I didn't do it. Honest I didn't. I swear.' I spoke before either of them had a chance.

'It says here . . .'

'I didn't do it . . .'

'It says here,' Dad continued firmly, 'that you hacked into Mrs Bracken's PC account and read the maths file.'

Mum was shaking her head at me as Dad spoke. Both their faces were stern, grim.

'You've already made up your minds that I did it, haven't you?' I shouted at them. 'You don't believe me, do you? You'd believe me if I were Gib.'

'And just what does that mean, young lady?' Mum's voice was ice cold.

149

'You haven't even heard my side yet but I'm guilty,' I screamed at her. And suddenly all the hurt and anger that I'd been through over the last few days came flooding out of my mouth. 'I bet you'd believe me if I was your real daughter. My real mum and dad would have believed me . . .'

Silence.

I don't know who was more stunned at my words – me or Mum and Dad. I hadn't meant to say that. I don't know where it came from. Then again, maybe I did . . .

Now that the words were out, they hung between us like a curtain. Something warm and salty ran into my mouth. Only then did I realize I was crying.

'Victoria, how could you say that?' Mum said quietly. 'If you say you didn't do it, then we believe you.'

'No you don't,' I sniffed. 'I saw the look on your faces.'

'You're not being fair, Victoria,' Dad began.

'Yes I am,' I argued. 'You read Miss Hiff's letter and made up your minds instantly. Well, it wasn't me. I know who really did do it and it wasn't me.'

'I think we all need to calm down, Victoria,' Dad said. 'I think you should go to your room.'

'With pleasure,' I retorted.

I ran out of the room and upstairs. Dad didn't call after me to walk not run. That made me feel worse. Gib was on the landing at the top of the stairs, listening. He stood back when he saw me. I ran past him into my room, slamming the door shut. I threw myself down on the bed, burying my face in my pillow. Giving Mum and Dad the headmistress's letter hadn't gone the way I'd wanted it to go at all. I'd spent all afternoon rehearsing what I would say and how I would say it, but when the moment had arrived . . .

Why was nothing ever simple? I stood up and got out the photograph of my real mum and dad from my sock drawer. I returned to my bed and lay down on my back, holding the photograph out in front of me. I felt so lonely.

A few minutes later there was a knock at my door. I ignored it, hoping whoever it was would go away.

'Can I come in?' Dad popped his head around the door.

I nodded reluctantly.

Dad came into my room, carefully closing the door behind him. I sat up but I couldn't look at him. I stared down at my duvet instead. Dad hovered in the middle of the room.

'Victoria . . . your mum and I are worried about you,' Dad began.

'Why?' I mumbled. 'I'm all right.'

'But you're obviously not. Have all my problems with the bank made you angry with us, with me?'

Shocked, I looked up. 'No! No, of course not.'

'Then what's the matter?'

I shrugged, looking down again. Nervously, I laced the duvet in and out between my fingers.

'Do you mind if I sit?' Dad asked.

I shook my head. I felt the end of the bed sink as Dad sat down heavily, but I still couldn't look at him.

'I know that sometimes it's difficult for you, Victoria,' Dad said softly. 'I know sometimes you feel a bit like a sore thumb, especially when people see you with your mum and start staring at you. But I want to say one thing. As far as your mum and I are concerned you *are* our daughter, as if you were born to us. Sometimes we have a job to remember that you weren't. But it makes no difference to how we feel about you. So that's how we treat you, like our daughter, 'cause that's who you are. And if you think we don't treat you like that then you're wrong. Dead wrong. Do you understand, Victoria?'

'Dad . . .' I began tentatively. How should I put this? 'Dad, are you and Mum sometimes sorry you adopted me?'

'Never,' Dad replied immediately. 'Never, ever.'

'Why . . . why did you adopt me?' I asked, my head still bent.

'Well . . .' Dad began slowly. 'We had our names down to be foster parents and when your parents were killed and it was found out that you had no close relatives, the social services asked us if we would foster you. And of course, once we'd seen you, there was no way we could give you back, even when we un-expectedly discovered that Laura was pregnant with Gib. So we applied to adopt you.'

'Oh, I see,' I said. 'Weren't you s-sorry when you knew you were going to have Gib?'

'Of course not,' Dad said. 'We thought and still think we're the luckiest people in the world.'

'I bet lots of people told you not to adopt me,' I whispered.

'One or two people. Laura and I soon told them where to go. Your Aunt Beth was one of the few people who understood our decision. She was great. She really supported your mum and me.' Dad smiled. 'Victoria, you can't go through life trying to please everyone. You'd never do it — it's impossible. You just end up pleasing no one. So you just have to please yourself.'

Maybe that was my problem. Maybe *I* was trying to please too many people. Gib and Chaucy, Maggie and Gayle. And in trying to please everyone, I'd end up pleasing no one.

'All right then,' Dad said, his tone of voice changing to become more firm. 'Now, tell me all about this maths-exam business. From the beginning.'

Picking my way carefully through the words, I told him — leaving out the bit about opening the letter! I implied that Miss Hiff had told me what I was supposed to be guilty of in her office.

'You said downstairs that you know who the real culprit is,' Dad said when I'd finished.

'Yeah, I guess . . .'

'Are you guessing or do you know?' Dad asked sternly.

'I know.'

'Who is it?'

'I can't tell you.'

'It's someone you know from school?' Dad asked after a moment's silence.

'Yes . . .'

'A friend . . . ?'

'She's not my friend any more,' I sighed. 'I told her that if she didn't tell Miss Hiff the truth then I would.'

'And are you going to?' Dad asked.

Slowly, I shook my head.

'Victoria, I can understand that you don't want to tell tales but . . .'

'I can't tell you, Dad. I just can't,' I pleaded.

Dad frowned.

'Why does Miss Hiff say in her letter that you admitted to breaking into Mrs Bracken's answer file?' Dad asked, after a moment's pause.

''Cause she asked me if I'd got the answers by using a program and I did.'

'Oh?'

'I used the programmable calculator you and Mum bought me for Christmas to get the answers,' I said reluctantly.

'You wrote a program on it?' Dad asked.

'That's right. And when she asked me, I thought she was talking about writing a program on that . . .'

'When instead she was talking about Mrs Bracken's PC,' Dad concluded.

I nodded.

'Victoria, you know you shouldn't have used your calculator like that in a maths exam,' Dad said. 'That's not why we bought it for you.'

'I know. I just thought . . . I thought I was being clever,' I admitted. 'It didn't occur to me until Crackly Bracken went nuclear that I maybe shouldn't have done it.'

Dad's lips twitched.

'There's no "maybe" about it. You shouldn't have done it. I trust you're not going to do it again?'

'No fear,' I replied instantly.

'Right! I'm down that school first thing tomorrow morning to get this sorted out.' Dad stood up. 'Now you finish your homework and then come downstairs and I'll give you a game of chess.'

He walked to the door.

'Dad, was Mum . . . was Mum upset?' I had to know.

Dad said, 'A little, but she'll be all right.'

'I . . . I'm sorry,' I whispered.

'That's OK, pumpkin,' he said. 'You wouldn't be my daughter if you didn't get strange ideas sometimes.'

I smiled as he left the room. I felt a lot better now I'd

had a proper talk with Dad. No sooner did my bedroom door shut, than it opened again.

'Hi, Vicky, are you OK?' Gib asked, hovering just inside the door.

'Yeah, I'm fine. What do you want?' I asked ungraciously.

'You said you had an idea about how to prove Eric's the crook, not Dad,' Gib replied.

I sighed. Would it kill Gib to say he was sorry – just once? If he ever apologized to me – for anything – I would pass out from severe shock.

'I was thinking about it today,' I said, bouncing off the bed. 'I reckon I've worked out why the date and time of the TIMETRV object file are a whole day after the program got linked.'

'I'm listening.' Gib came into the room and sat down in my chair. I sat at the edge of my bed.

'Well, I was thinking about how I'd try to get money from the bank,' I said eagerly. 'If I didn't have access to the cashiers' user accounts and I could write a program to do it, I reckon it would be quite simple – if I knew exactly what I was doing.'

'Go on.'

'I'd change a noddy program days before it was needed, to contain one of those time-trap things Dad was talking about. One of the programs that runs every night. Then, on a certain day at a certain time, the money would get transferred.'

'I get you,' Gib said, leaning forward. 'But how would you get round the acceptance testers? They check all the source programs to make sure there's nothing in them that shouldn't be there.'

'Ah, but suppose I changed a noddy program that did something pretty boring to include the time-trap code I wanted, to transfer money about? I could compile it so I'd have an object file, then re-edit the source code to take my time-trap code out.'

'And that's what you'd give to the acceptance testers . . .' Gib said with a slow smile. He always was fast on the uptake.

'Exactly! I'd wait for them to check the source program and compile it, and then I'd overwrite their object file which doesn't contain the time-trap . . .'

'With your object file which does.'

Gib and I smiled at each other.

'And it'd be that object file that they linked and ran. Of course, they wouldn't see any sign of the time-trap because that bit of code wouldn't run until the date and time I'd already specified.'

'Very clever.' Gib whistled. 'But what about the object file? Why was it dated one day ahead of the linked file?'

'Think about it. You've fiddled about with all these files and you know they've all got different dates and times. The only file that you want left on the system that contains any of your time-trap program would be the linked file. So after TIMETRV has been linked, you then overwrite the object file with a clean version of the same thing. Then there's less chance of the fiddle being detected.'

'Except that the date of the object file is different in the batch library,' Gib pointed out.

'But who would notice that? Why would they even check that? Once it goes through the acceptance testers, all anyone cares about are the files on the live system, not the development system. And only the linked files get copied across to the live system,' I said, practically bouncing off the bed by this time.

'And if it wasn't for you printing off the batch library file on the development system accidentally . . .' Gib grinned.

'And your brilliant eyesight,' I beamed.

'Then no one would be any the wiser,' Gib said. 'That's terrific!'

'That has to be the way it was done,' I said. 'Don't you think?'

'I don't see any other way it could be done,' Gib agreed.

For the first time in ages, I actually began to feel good. We were getting closer and closer all the time. I felt sure that that was how it was done. I couldn't help feeling a bit clever.

Then my smile faded. 'Now that brings us to Eric and *why* he put that million pounds in Dad's account.'

'Do you think more than the million was taken?' Gib asked.

'I'm sure of it,' I frowned. 'The thing is, why hasn't the bank discovered more missing money yet?'

'They knew pretty quickly that Dad had the money in his account,' Gib said.

'And we must be talking about an awful lot of money being taken out if Eric can stick one million pounds into Dad's account, just like that,' I said.

'Not yet . . .' Gib said slowly.

'Pardon!'

'Maybe the rest of the money, the real money that Eric was after, hasn't been transferred *yet*.' Gib's eyes sparkled.

'Of course,' I breathed. 'If you can set up one time-trap, why not set up two? That way you get the bank chasing in the wrong direction until it's too late.'

'So Eric put the money in Dad's account just to get the bank going round in circles.'

'It's more than that. I think he didn't want Dad's checking program to run either. He must've been afraid that it would pick up something.'

'The way we did,' Gib said.

I nodded.

'So what about Eric and our proof?' Gib asked.

'I need a PC to find any,' I sighed. 'This is pure speculation. And if we did tell Dad and the bank, Eric

159

could cover his tracks with no trouble at all. Then Dad would still be in trouble.'

'Where are you going to find a PC?' Gib asked. 'The ones at school are out. The computer club is on tomorrow lunchtime and the computing evening classes will be running tomorrow night. Unless we try to get into the school in the early hours of the morning.'

'I don't fancy that much.' I grimaced.

'To tell the truth, neither do I,' Gib admitted.

That made me feel a whole lot better.

'So what do we do?'

Our heads in our hands, Gib and I gave it some serious thought. Then I had the best idea I'd had all year.

'Gib, Aunt Beth's got a PC – she can log onto the bank's computer from home the same way Dad can.' I sprang off the bed.

'She'll let us borrow it – no problems,' Gib said enthusiastically.

'But we can't tell her why we want to use it,' I said fiercely. 'That's between you and me until we have something Dad can take to the police about his so-called friend, Eric.'

I didn't want Gib to get any funny ideas.

'All right! Don't take my head off,' Gib protested. 'When should we ask her?'

'We'll pop round tomorrow, after school,' I said.

Gib frowned. 'But aren't she and Sebastian going to Rio the day after?'

'So?'

'They'll be busy packing and stuff.'

'They're not going to pack the PC,' I said. 'And we'll tell them we'll be quick. We can use the same home-work excuse you used with Rosa, the evening-class tutor.'

'Yeah, it was good, wasn't it!' Gib said modestly.

I ducked down.

'What're you doing?' Gib asked curiously.

'Just trying to get out of the way of your big head,' I told him.

Gib laughed. 'You're just jealous,' he replied. 'Right then. Let's get this sorted. We'll meet up at the school gates after school and go to Aunt Beth's together.'

I grinned. 'You're on. Tomorrow night, we're going to get Eric, good and proper. Once and for all!'

Chapter Eleven

EJONES

'Are you going to be excluded then?' Gib asked.

It was after school and Gib and I were walking to Aunt Beth's house. It was a strange day – one of those days when it rained on and off. But that didn't stop the sky from being mostly blue and the sun from shining anyway. I, for one, was glad school was over. Dad had embarrassed me something awful.

'If my daughter said she didn't do it, then she didn't do it . . . are you accusing my daughter of telling lies . . . ? Of course, Victoria's calculator is programmable. I bought it for her myself . . . are you telling me what I should and shouldn't buy my own daughter . . . ?' And all the time I'd just been sinking lower and lower into my chair. Miss Hiff made me show her how I'd worked out my program. Then she'd tried out the program on my calculator herself. After that, she looked like she wasn't sure what to think. But that worked in my favour.

'For your information,' I told Gib loftily, 'I got a

week's detention for writing a program to do what I should have worked out in my head.'

'So she believed you?' Gib said.

'Of course. She had to. Dad wouldn't let her do anything else.'

Gib smiled.

'And I didn't even have to drop Maggie in it,' I went on.

'Maggie?' Gib frowned. 'What's Maggie got to do with this?'

I looked at Gib. 'This is between you and me – right? Maggie's the one who hacked into Mrs Bracken's exam file to get the answers. She's going through a lot at home right now and she didn't have a chance to revise properly.'

'That's no excuse for dropping you in it,' Gib said with gratifying indignation.

'I don't think she meant to. I just happened to be showing off that I'd finished the exam when Crackly Bracken was looking around to see who finished before everyone else.'

'Even so . . .'

'It doesn't matter. It's sorted out now. I'm to get a week's worth of detention and that's it,' I interrupted. 'I'm just glad it's over with. Now Maggie needn't try to turn everyone against me.'

'What d'you mean? Is that what she threatened you with if you told anyone?'

I nodded.

'You wait. I'll sort her out,' Gib muttered.

I looked at Gib and laughed. 'My hero!' I teased.

The tips of Gib's ears went bright red, which made me laugh even more. He'd never stuck up for me before. I kind of liked it!

'Hi, Aunt Beth. How are you?'

'Hello, Aunt Beth.'

'Gib, Vicky, what on earth are you doing here?'

The puzzled frown on Aunt Beth's face wasn't very flattering, to say the least. In fact, she looked almost unwelcoming.

'Can we use your PC for our computing home-work?' I asked. 'Mum said that if you didn't mind, then we could.'

'Why didn't you phone me first?' Aunt Beth asked. There was no mistaking the impatient tone in her voice.

'Er . . . we tried phoning you at lunchtime but your phone was engaged,' Gib told her. 'We thought we'd take the chance and come straight from school.'

Aunt Beth frowned down at both of us. She looked like she was sucking on a lemon.

'I wish you hadn't,' she said bluntly. 'We're right in the middle of packing and the house is a mess. I don't know whether I'm . . .'

'Beth, who is it?'

Sebastian emerged from the shadows and foliage of

the hall to stand behind Aunt Beth. His steel-blue eyes looked surprised then strangely guarded as he looked at us. When he wasn't smiling he looked totally different. Very serious and reserved.

'What brings you two here?' he asked.

I was glad Gib was standing beside me. All of a sudden I felt very nervous.

'Er . . . em . . . Sebastian, we were wondering if we could use your PC?' Gib said. 'It's for our homework which has got to be in tomorrow. Dad doesn't have a PC any more . . . It won't take long. An hour at the most.'

'We're packing,' Sebastian said.

'We won't disturb you,' Gib persisted. 'Honest we won't. *Please.*'

'And it'll only take an hour?' Aunt Beth said.

'That's right,' we both said.

Aunt Beth and Sebastian looked at each other for several moments. I nudged Gib with my elbow. I didn't like this. We were obviously intruding.

'OK, you two can use it,' Aunt Beth said, with a reluctant smile, 'but I do wish you'd phoned first. Sebastian, why don't you go upstairs and prepare it for them?'

'That's all right, Aunt Beth,' I began. 'We can do that.'

'Oh no, I insist,' Aunt Beth argued.

After directing an irritated look at Beth, Sebastian bounded up the stairs like some great, ungainly dog.

165

'Come and have a drink first.' Aunt Beth steered us into the hall and straight into the kitchen.

'We don't want to put you to any trouble,' I said.

'It's no trouble,' Aunt Beth replied, her tone telling us that if that was our wish, then we had failed.

Aunt Beth poured out two glasses of milk. I ask you! Milk! After pulling a face at Gib, I pretended to sip at mine. The smell alone was enough to make me want to gag! We stood and sipped in silence. No one seemed to have anything to say.

'I'm afraid we don't have any fruit juice. Sebastian and I didn't go shopping this week because we're leaving for Rio tomorrow. The milk came from the shop around the corner.'

Don't they sell fruit juice then? I thought without saying it.

'How's your dad?' Aunt Beth asked after another pause.

I shrugged.

'He's fine,' Gib replied.

'Has anything turned up yet?' Aunt Beth asked.

We both shook our heads.

'Not yet,' said Gib.

'I'm sure it will,' Aunt Beth smiled. 'You're not drinking, Vicky.'

'I thought I'd save it for when I was working upstairs.' I said the first thing that came into my head. Not bad! I thought.

'You two can use the PC now.'

Sebastian's voice from the kitchen door made me jump. I hadn't even heard him come downstairs. He seemed to fill the whole doorway, lengthways that is. He was as skinny as a piece of string but really tall. I could only vaguely remember Aunt Beth's first husband and Sebastian was nothing like him.

'Come on, Vicky.' Gib grabbed me by the arm. 'Thanks, Aunt Beth. It's really kind of you.'

'Yeah, thanks,' I repeated.

'You can use the PC room and the bathroom – and that's it,' Sebastian said as we passed him. 'The other rooms are tips and I don't want them disturbed until our packing is finished.'

I turned round to frown at him. 'We weren't going to go anywhere else.'

'Fair enough,' Sebastian replied with a smile.

I followed Gib out into the hall.

'Here! Hold that, Gib.' I gave him my glass of milk. Then I took off my jacket and hung it up over the banisters.

Gib handed my milk back to me and we both walked upstairs. The back bedroom with the PC in it was the only upstairs room which had the door open. All the other bedroom doors were closed – obviously deliberately.

'Does he think we're going to run off with his wardrobe or something?' I whispered to Gib.

167

'Come on. We're obviously interrupting them so the sooner we start, the sooner we'll finish,' Gib whispered back.

I sat down at the PC and switched it on. Whatever it was that Sebastian had been preparing upstairs, it certainly hadn't been the computer.

'Here, Gib, could you chuck this away for me?' I asked, handing him my milk.

While Gib went to the bathroom with his glass and mine, I fished Dad's memory stick out of my school bag and started running the comms program. By the time Gib came back I was through to the Universal Bank network system.

'I don't suppose you could do me another favour?' I asked Gib hopefully.

'What?'

'That milk has left a nasty taste in my mouth,' I said. 'I don't suppose you could pop to the shop around the corner and get me a fruit smoothie or a ginger beer or something? Anything but cola.'

'Oh, all right,' Gib said reluctantly.

It was just as well I was sitting down! I gawped at Gib. 'You mean you're going to do it!'

'Just this once,' Gib said firmly. 'So don't push your luck.'

I kept my mouth shut, not wanting to spoil it. He was actually going to do it. If I'd had a diary I would have noted this day down for sure.

Once Gib left I tried logging on to the System Manager's user account on the development machine, hoping it'd have the same 'cabbage' password it had on the live system. I was in luck. It did. Suddenly everything was going right.

'I'm just going to the shop at the bottom of the road,' I heard Gib tell Aunt Beth downstairs.

I frowned at the PC screen. Something was bothering me and I couldn't for the life of me figure out what it was. I wanted to type out the staff file again, just to make sure that we hadn't missed anything. Then I needed to double-check the *ejones* account. I wanted to make sure there'd be no holes in the proof Gib and I presented to Dad and the police. No way was Eric going to wriggle his way out of this one. I typed out the staff file, stopping the screen when it got to the Js.

Then I knew what had been troubling me.

Eric's account was the Systems Manager's account. The user name for that account was SYSTEM not *ejones*. He must have set up the *ejones* account on the sly. Better and better. If he had, then it'd be easier to prove that he and only he could have changed the TIMETRV program. So now to check the *ejones* account.

I typed:

SYSTEM>DISPLAYSTAFFILE/BRIEF/USER NAME=EJONES

Then *ejones* appeared on the screen.

'Yes!' I clenched my fists and punched the air above my head. Closer and closer . . . But I needed more than just the user name played back to me. I chewed on my bottom lip until I realized what I'd done wrong. I typed:

>DISPLAY STAFFILE/FULL/USERNAME=EJONES

I decided I might as well get a list of all the privileges Eric had assigned himself, as well as his full system name and a summary of all the other information held for his account. I pressed the enter key and the information I wanted appeared on the screen. Unable to believe my eyes, I stared at it. I thought I was going crazy. I *had* to be going crazy. But there it was in big, pixellated letters. There were about five lines of data but all I was interested in were the top two. I checked, double-checked and triple-checked the lines to make sure I'd typed in the user name correctly.

>EJONES: JONES, ELIZABETH JANINE: SYSTEM:
   ACCOUNT_LINK=CARTER, BETH

Elizabeth Janine Jones? The account link was to Aunt Beth's user account. That meant once Aunt Beth had logged on using her 'Beth Carter' account, she could then log on again as *ejones*. And hers was the only account link. The *ejones* account had to belong to Aunt Beth.

But it couldn't. I didn't understand at all.

All at once, the hairs on my nape started to tickle and prickle. I rubbed the back of my neck but the feeling wouldn't go away. Then my blood turned ice cold. I turned quickly – and there was Sebastian, standing right behind me.

Chapter Twelve

Locked Up

'I just knew we shouldn't have let you in here.'

I couldn't move. I couldn't even blink. I just stared up at Sebastian, horrified.

'I knew you were up to something.' Sebastian scowled at me. 'What kid is that keen to do their homework? But Beth wouldn't listen to me, would she. Now what are we going to do with you?'

And the look on his face clinched it. There was no mistake.

'Aunt Beth and *ejones* are one and the same person . . . You're the ones who did this to Dad . . .' I whispered. Even though I knew it was true, I still couldn't believe it. 'You just wait till I tell Mum and Dad. You rotten, stinking . . .'

'So they don't know yet . . .' Sebastian smiled at me. A smile that made my whole body tremble.

I could've bitten off my tongue. My mouth was the size of the Channel Tunnel at the best of times, but now I'd really surpassed myself. *Aunt Beth and Sebastian . . .*

'Why Jones? I don't understand that bit,' I said.

Stay calm and keep talking, Victoria, I told myself. I had to figure a way out of this.

'So you don't know everything, you egg-headed little snoop.' Sebastian folded his arms across his chest.

'I know you and Aunt Beth set up my dad,' I said furiously, all my thoughts about keeping calm flying out of the window. 'I know Aunt Beth doctored the TIMETRV file to put one million pounds in Dad's account, and I know she's probably transferring money into one of your accounts tonight, ready for skipping off to Rio tomorrow. I'm not stupid, you know.'

'No, you're not, are you? In fact, you're too clever for your own good, Victoria,' Sebastian said softly.

I was in deep, *deep* trouble.

'So why Jones?' I asked again, desperate to keep Sebastian talking while I worked out my escape route.

'Jones was Beth's maiden name before she married,' Sebastian said. 'The bank's previous Systems Manager decided it would be easier to create a new user account for Beth when she married for the first time, instead of modifying the old one. We discovered the old account by accident. It came in very useful, very useful indeed. And no one knew about it – until now.'

The doorbell rang. I made a break for the stairs.

'Gib! GIB!' I screamed.

A warm, sweaty hand was clamped over my mouth. I was lifted off the ground. I kicked and punched and scratched at Sebastian's arms but he wouldn't let me go. He carried me out on to the landing.

'Sebastian, what's going on?' Aunt Beth was at the top of the stairs. The doorbell rang again.

'She knows,' Sebastian said.

Aunt Beth looked from Sebastian to me and back again. Her eyes narrowed and turned stone cold, stone hard. I tried to bite Sebastian's fingers which were still over my mouth, but I couldn't get a grip.

'Gi . . . mmm . . . Gi . . .' My shout was totally muffled by Sebastian's fingers.

'Beth, do something. They could ruin everything. You've got to get rid of her brother,' Sebastian hissed.

'How do I do that?' Aunt Beth said urgently.

'Think of something,' snapped Sebastian.

'Gi . . . Gi . . .'

Her forehead furrowed, Aunt Beth went back downstairs. Sebastian dragged me back into the bedroom with the PC. I kicked and struggled furiously every millimetre of the way, but it was no good.

'Hiya, Aunt Beth. I . . .'

'Oh! Hello, Gib.' Aunt Beth sounded surprised. 'Didn't you pass Vicky on your way back here?'

'Pass her?'

'She didn't feel well all of a sudden, so she decided to go home.'

'I didn't see her,' I heard Gib say.

Frantically, I struggled as Sebastian held me, but I

174

couldn't get him to let me go. His hand clamped even tighter over my mouth. I was burning hot and I could hardly breathe.

'You must have just missed each other,' Aunt Beth said.

'Yeah, we must have,' Gib said slowly.

'Gi . . . Gi . . .' I wriggled in Sebastian's grasp but I couldn't get the words out.

'OK. 'Bye, Aunt Beth,' Gib said.

'NO! Don't go!' I screamed inside.

''Bye, Gib.'

I heard the front door close.

Sebastian let go of me so suddenly, my legs almost collapsed under me. If it wasn't for him holding onto my arms, I would have fallen. Aunt Beth came running up the stairs.

'You just wait – both of you. You'll get what you deserve!' I shouted, still struggling to get free.

'Not from you, you little snot,' Sebastian said from behind me. 'If you think we're going to miss out on seven million quid 'cause of you.'

Seven million . . . I turned my head to stare at him.

'Something else you didn't know,' Sebastian said icily.

'What do we do now?' Aunt Beth asked, glaring at me. 'When Gib gets to his house, he'll know we were lying.'

'Get on the phone and speak to his mum and dad,' Sebastian said. 'Tell them that Vicky did leave but then

175

came back here rather than walk all the way home. Tell them we'll look after her so she'll be sleeping here tonight.'

'What about Vicky going to school tomorrow? We can't let her go until we're out of the country,' Aunt Beth said.

'By the time anyone knows she's missing tomorrow, we'll be long gone. Let's just make sure David and Laura don't come knocking at our front door tonight,' Sebastian said.

'You wicked cow!' I yelled at Aunt Beth. 'You're supposed to be Mum and Dad's friend. You're both supposed to be Mum and Dad's friends. You just wait . . .'

'No friendship is worth seven million pounds.' Sebastian smiled like the Cheshire cat at me.

'You skunk! You rotten toad! You'll get yours,' I hissed at him.

'I never meant for your father to get involved but he was snooping. He was getting much too close. And then there was that checking program of his,' Aunt Beth said. 'I'm sorry it had to be David, I really am.'

If I could just get at her for a few seconds. I wanted to tear her hair out.

'What do we do with her?' Aunt Beth eyed me as if I was something unpleasant she'd just stepped in.

'She can stay locked up until we leave for Rio,' Sebastian replied.

'Sebastian, I'm not sure . . .'

'If we let her go, she'll go straight to her mum and dad or the police. Do you want that?'

Aunt Beth frowned for a moment. She shook her head, then turned to walk downstairs. Sebastian half pulled, half carried me after her.

'You just wait – both of you!' I shouted again, struggling all the time.

Aunt Beth led the way into the kitchen and opened a door. Gloom and a stale, musty smell seeped out into the kitchen. There was a brick wall about a metre behind the door, and I thought it was a cupboard, but then I saw the few steps which led down to the cellar.

'Give me your phone,' demanded Beth.

I thought about denying I had it, but Beth knew very well that I carried it everywhere because it had my music on it. Sebastian's eyes narrowed like he was daring me to deny I had it, so I reluctantly handed it over. Then Sebastian shoved me through the door, before slamming it shut behind me. Turning quickly, I tried to push open the door but I heard the bolt slide home. It was pitch black and smelt dusty and foul. I banged on the door with my fists.

'Let me out! Let me out this minute!' I shouted.

'Phone from upstairs or they might hear her shouting,' I heard Sebastian say.

I banged even louder until the sides of my hands were aching. I was sure I must have broken every bone

177

in them, but still I hammered on the cellar door. Then I had an idea. I backed up as far as I could before charging like a demented bull for the cellar door, shoulder first – like in the movies. It hurt like blazes!

'I won't do that again,' I mumbled, rubbing my shoulder.

Gingerly, I felt around for a light switch or light cord or something. My fingers met with something stringy and fine. A spider's web! I screamed, wiping my fingers on my jeans. I hate spiders. I felt around again. My fingers touched what felt like a piece of string hanging down.

It's too sturdy to be another spider's web, I thought, hope rising up like a flare inside me.

I pulled at the string. The sudden light blinded me, making me blink rapidly. I looked around. Wooden steps led down into a small room, half hidden by long shadows. I ran down the steps. Perhaps there was another way out. Once down there, I saw that there wasn't even a window, never mind a door. The cellar was tiny, about twice the size of a broom cupboard. A tatty anorak and a long scarf hung from the coat hooks attached to the wall on my right. The floor was covered with stone tiles. There were cobwebs everywhere – over the old, broken bits of furniture, in the corners, even over the small, empty wine-rack which stood against one wall. Looking down to my left, I saw a lever (gas?), a couple of meters and an electricity fuse-box. I sneezed, then sneezed again. The dust was getting up my nose. That was it! No way was I going to stay in there all night.

'LET ME OUT!' I shouted. I ran up the stairs and pounded on the door again.

That didn't last long. My hands were hurting too much to keep it up. I listened, but couldn't hear a thing.

Locked up. I was really locked up! In a musty, dusty cellar. And I had no idea when – or even if – I'd be let out. I sat down on the top step and rubbed my battered hands.

'You just wait, Sebastian,' I muttered. Before, I'd been more angry than scared but now that was beginning to change.

'Gib, where are you?' I whispered. 'Someone, *anyone*, where are you?'

An hour later, I was banging on the cellar door again.

'Let me out! I need to go to the loo!' I shouted.

Nothing. Not a word, not a sound. Sebastian and Aunt Beth wouldn't go out and leave me, would they? I battered even harder at the door.

'I'm not joking. I need to go to the loo. I'm busting!' I shouted.

Still no answer.

My hands were throbbing by now. I had to find something to beat at the door with. My hands couldn't take any more. I walked slowly down the stairs again. There had to be some way of getting them to let me out.

Come on Vicky, think, I told myself.

Then I saw it. The electricity fuse-box . . . I stared at it, a mega-brilliant idea forming. Normally, I wouldn't touch the thing. Electricity scared me and the thought of getting fried didn't appeal at all, but I'd once seen Mum turn off the electricity throughout our house when she wanted to change our living-room dimmer switch that had packed up. I squatted down to look at the fuse-box. There were several detachable fuses that I didn't like the look of and a large on/off switch to the right of the fuses.

I wasn't sure about this, but then my bladder made up my mind for me. I really did need to go! Taking a deep breath, I flicked up the on/off switch. Instantly the cellar was totally dark. I'd forgotten that I'd be in the dark too. I felt my way to the stairs and groped my way up them. It was so dark, it felt like being swallowed whole. I tried to hold on to my courage, as well as other things.

Within moments, I heard footsteps in the kitchen outside the cellar door. I waited as I heard the door bolt being drawn back. The door flew open and a pale yellow circle of light from a torch shone straight into my face.

'I need to go to the loo,' I repeated.

'What have you done?' Aunt Beth asked furiously.

Behind her I could make out the shadowy figure of Sebastian. He looked even more long and thin and weird in the dark – and that was saying something.

'She's turned off the electricity,' Sebastian said furiously. He pushed me out of the way and went down to turn the lights back on. This time I closed my eyes against the sudden light, opening them slowly after a few seconds.

'You do that again and you'll be sorry.' Sebastian pointed his finger at me.

'If you don't let me go to the toilet, then you're the ones who will be sorry,' I declared.

Aunt Beth took me by the arm, her fingers like pincers and pulled me upstairs. Sebastian followed us. I could feel his glaring eyes boring into my back. I wiped my hand over my sweaty forehead, but I didn't turn around. Once in the bathroom I locked the door.

'Don't think of trying any funny stuff,' Aunt Beth called after me. 'I can unlock the door from this side and the bit of the window that does open is far too small for you to get through.'

So much for that idea! I looked around. The two windows were both made with thick frosted glass and double-glazed at that. There were tiny slatted openings at the top of each window but that was it. The only way I could get through them was by turning into some kind of insect.

Minutes later I opened the door.

'I'm not going back in that cellar again. I don't care what you do,' I said. 'It's cold and full of spiders and it stinks.'

'You'll go where we put you,' Aunt Beth said.

'Not in the cellar I won't,' I argued, my muscles tensing. 'If you put me back in there, I'll keep turning the electricity off.'

Sebastian emerged from their bedroom.

'Oh no you won't. Not if you want to see your family again,' Sebastian said silkily.

I stared at him. 'You can't keep me in the cellar the whole night,' I protested.

'Watch us,' Sebastian retorted. 'We're not going to let you ruin the sweetest plan anyone's had this century. Not now we've come so far.'

'When we get to Rio and we're safe, I'll phone your parents and tell them where you are, but until then, the cellar is your home,' said Aunt Beth.

'You're not going to leave me locked up until you get to Rio, are you?' I asked, aghast.

'We've got no choice,' Aunt Beth said. 'Why didn't you keep your nose out of it, Victoria? Your dad would have been cleared once Sebastian and I got to Rio, I would have seen to that.'

Sebastian muttered under his breath.

It sounded like 'If I had my way . . .'

It's now or never, I thought.

I made a break for it, rushing between Aunt Beth and Sebastian to leg it downstairs. I got halfway down before Sebastian's vice-like fingers grabbed hold of my arm.

'Where do you think you're going?' he hissed.

He shoved me downstairs and back into the cellar. I pushed at the door as Sebastian locked it.

'YOU JUST WAIT!' I shouted, wishing I could think of something more threatening to say.

'No more tricks with the electricity meter or you can rot in there,' Sebastian warned. 'The only part of you anyone will ever find is your skeleton.'

I rubbed my arm where Sebastian had dug into me with his fingers. I'd have bruises there tomorrow but that was the least of my worries. I looked around. There had to be something I could do.

Think, Victoria, I told myself sternly.

I wasn't getting very far. Closing my eyes with frustration, I flopped down onto the top step and tried to think about what I should do next. But the only thought in my head was that I was in major trouble. Deep, *deep* trouble, Again!

'Don't just sit here! Do something!' I told myself sternly.

I searched for something with which to pry open the cellar door. There were lots of models of stupid planes and tanks and some of the biggest spiders I'd ever seen in my life, but precious little else. The few old bits of furniture I picked up crumbled in my hands. Furiously, I went back up to the door and pushed and pounded on it and shouted until my throat hurt and my hands ached and I was hoarse.

I got precisely nowhere.

On each hour and half hour, I tried banging on the door again, but I knew that was more for my benefit than anyone else's.

It was Aunt Beth and Sebastian all the time. My head was spinning. We'd got it completely wrong. Aunt Beth and Sebastian had set up my dad. I had to do something. I just had to. But what?

At last, exhausted, I sat down, my back against the door. And I cried myself to sleep.

When I woke up, it took me several seconds to remember where I was. I stood up abruptly, knocking my head against the door handle.

'A great way to start the day!' I grimaced, rubbing my head.

I pulled the light cord to switch off the lights. It was like trying to look through black ink. I couldn't tell if it was daylight or dark outside. And it was so quiet. I pulled the cord again, as much to hear the click it made as to switch the light back on.

From my muzzy, pounding head, I knew I'd slept for a good few hours – and not very well. I tried to shake out my legs and arms but I felt stiff as cardboard all over and my mouth felt like the bottom of a bird cage. I was dying for a glass of water. I tried the door. Still locked. I glanced down at my watch, wondering how long I'd slept. It was ten to eight. I looked, then stared at it.

Ten to eight in the morning? I couldn't have slept

that long. But I must have. Seeing it was daytime by my watch but not seeing any daylight made me feel much worse. It was as if I could no longer half convince myself that I was dreaming and would wake up any second. This was real. I was seconds away from panicking. The only thing that stopped me was that I was cold and uncomfortable and growing more and more angry by the second. How could I have fallen asleep?

I couldn't stay here all day, I just couldn't. Aunt Beth and Sebastian were leaving for Rio soon and if I didn't stop them, they'd get clean away.

I pushed at the cellar door. 'Help me! Please, help me!' I screamed, over and over.

I hammered on the door again. Minutes passed. It was no use. Neither Sebastian nor Aunt Beth came to tell me to shut up. I wondered if they had left the house already. I thought about the electricity fuse-box. That was one way to find out . . . But turning it off now might not do any good. They wouldn't need lights during the day and they'd probably already had their breakfast. But I had nothing to lose. Face set, I ran downstairs and flicked the electricity switch to 'off'. Darkness swallowed me up again. I clambered up the stairs, knowing I wouldn't be able to stand the darkness for too long.

'Let me out . . . right this second!' I started banging on the door again. Over and over. I began to feel like I was being smothered, suffocated. I *had* to get out.

The door opened so suddenly, I almost fell flat on my face. The sudden daylight overwhelmed me, making me blink rapidly. I lashed out blindly, determined to get away from Sebastian and Aunt Beth.

'Vicky, it's me!' Gib ducked my flailing arms.

I blinked and focused for the first time. There, standing in front of me was my scabby, ugly brother, who'd never looked better in his life.

'Gib! Am I glad to see you,' I said tearfully. 'I could kiss you!'

'I'd rather you didn't,' Gib said seriously.

I wanted to laugh and cry all at once. 'I've been locked up all night. I thought I'd never get out.' I swallowed hard past the huge lump in my throat. 'Where are Sebastian and Aunt Beth? Is it safe?'

'I waited until they both went out before sneaking in,' Gib said. 'What's going on? Why'd they . . .?'

'How did you manage to get in the house?' I interrupted. I looked around nervously, afraid Aunt Beth and Sebastian would appear at any second.

'I went round the back. I thought I'd have to break a window or something until I remembered where they keep their spare key. Do you remember when they were joking with Dad and Mum about keeping it in the shed at the bottom of their garden under those huge sacks of fertilizer. I'm glad I thought of it. I must admit, I didn't fancy a spot of breaking and entering. What's that? About five years in the nick?' Gib wrinkled up his nose.

I smiled shakily at Gib. I was beginning to feel a little less tearful.

'Why would they leave their key?' I sniffed.

'Well, you couldn't get at it so it wouldn't have done you much good,' Gib pointed out. 'Besides, I don't think they'll have much use for their kitchen-door key once they're in Rio. Vicky, are you all right?'

'Nothing a long, hot shower wouldn't sort out.' I tried to smile.

I felt smelly and dirty and I couldn't stop looking over my shoulder. Then I realized something. This was the first time Gib had ever asked me how I was feeling. Somehow just that made me feel better.

'Are you sure you're OK?'

'I'm fine,' I replied.

'I knew there was nothing wrong with you,' Gib said smugly.

'What d'you mean? I've been locked up in this grotty cellar all night,' I said with indignation.

'No, I was talking about that story Aunt Beth gave me last night – and I believed her. She phoned Mum and Dad to say you'd come back to her house and you'd be spending the night with them. She said that Sebastian would drop you off at school today,' Gib snorted. 'I didn't realize she was lying until I'd almost fallen asleep.'

'What made you realize?' I asked.

'Your jacket. I remembered that when Aunt Beth was telling me you'd gone home, your jacket was still over

187

the banister. She should have made sure I couldn't see it,' Gib told me.

I glared at him. 'If you realized she was lying, why didn't you tell Mum and Dad, you little squirt?'

'I was just about to, but then I started wondering why Aunt Beth had lied,' Gib began. 'I realized you must have found out something important. Something to do with Aunt Beth and Dad and Dad's bank. I thought long and hard about it but I reckoned you'd be safe – at least until they set off for Rio. They were obviously up to something and I didn't want to scare them off or warn them that I was on to them. Besides, I didn't know what they were up to, so what could I tell Mum and Dad that they would believe? I could hardly say that I thought they were kidnapping you! I wasn't to know they'd lock you up in the cellar all night.'

'True. But I still want to throttle you!' I scowled. 'I've been locked up in that spider trap for ages. It was horrible. Like being shut up in a coffin.'

'Stop moaning,' Gib ordered.

'What about Mum and Dad? Weren't they worried about me?'

Gib shrugged. 'They believed Aunt Beth's story about you not feeling well and wanting to stay at her house for the night. Mind you, Mum was all for coming round here to get you but Aunt Beth managed to dissuade her in the end.'

'I bet she did.' I frowned. 'Well, I'm not calling her Aunt Beth any more. She's no aunt of mine.'

I waited for Gib to say something clever about Aunt Beth not being my real aunt in the first place.

'She's no aunt of mine either. Lying and locking you up like that,' Gib replied. 'So what happened? Am I right? Did you find out something important?'

'I found out something all right. I found out that *ejones* stands for Elizabeth Janine Jones. Jones was Aunt Beth's, I mean Beth's maiden name before she got married the first time. That's why next to JONES, E in the staff file, the user name is given as SYSTEM. Eric doesn't have any other account but the SYSTEM account. He doesn't need any other account. And, of course, Aunt Beth's name wouldn't be down as *ejones* because that's not her name any more. She's down as *bcarter* – for Beth Carter. Not *ejones*. And do you know what they've done? She and Sebastian have fleeced seven million pounds from Universal Bank.'

'Seven million . . . You're joking,' Gib said, astounded.

'No I'm not. I just wish I knew what their next move was going to be. I don't know where they are. It's too early for them to be on their way to the airport. Their plane doesn't leave until four this afternoon.'

'Four o'clock? How do you know?'

'I saw it on their tickets,' I shrugged.

'Thank goodness for that,' Gib whistled. 'When they both left so early, I thought they might have a morning flight. We've still got some time then. Come on. Let's go home, you can get tidied up and then we'll go to school and wait for Chaucy there.'

'What about Mum and Dad? If we go home now, they'll want to know why we aren't at school,' I pointed out.

'Dad's taken Mum to the antenatal clinic. They'll be gone all morning,' Gib smiled.

'Hmm! And why do we have to wait for Chaucy? When did you speak to him?'

'Earlier this morning,' Gib said. 'His mum was a bit annoyed that I phoned so early, but she let me speak to him. I told him about you being here and that something strange was going on.'

'Did you have to do that?' I asked.

'Of course. I needed his help,' Gib replied, as if it was the most logical thing in the world. I almost envied him. He found it a lot easier to ask for help and confide in people than I did.

'His help with what?' I said.

'To follow Beth, of course,' Gib replied.

Chapter Thirteen

Hatton Something

'I don't understand. What d'you mean?' I asked, baffled.

'Well, Sebastian's car wasn't in front of the house when Chaucy and I got here, so we thought we'd had it. Then we saw Aunt Beth through the front-room window and, luckily for us, Sebastian turned up about ten minutes later. He went into the house and then he came out carrying one big suitcase and a little one. At first I was scared that they were both going to the airport for their flight to Rio and then what would we do? But Sebastian got into his car by himself and drove off. About ten minutes after that Aunt Beth . . . that is, Beth came out of the house. She walked off down the street and Chaucy followed her.'

'Why didn't you follow her?' I asked.

'I was going to until Chaucy pointed out that he had less chance of being spotted. Beth doesn't know him. Besides, someone had to see what had happened to you.'

'You needn't make it sound like you'd rather have had your toenails pulled out,' I sniffed.

'I'm here, aren't I?'

I couldn't argue with that. I smiled.

'Yeah, you are. Thanks! So where's Aunt Beth now?' I asked.

'How on earth am I supposed to know that?' Gib said. 'That's the whole reason why Chaucy's following her. We figured she was going somewhere first, before heading for the airport. He's got his mobile phone on him so I told him to phone me or you when he could.'

'Yeah, it was a stupid question,' I mumbled. 'Put it down to the rotten night I've just had!'

'Let's get cracking,' Gib said. 'We've got a lot to do.'

Yes we have, I thought. The only trouble was, Chaucy was doing most of it.

'Maybe we should phone the bank and at least tell them what Beth and Sebastian are doing,' I suggested.

'Oh yeah! Like they're going to believe you and me,' Gib scoffed. 'We're kids – and not just any kids, but David Gibson's kids. Of course they'll believe us!'

'I think we should at least try. We need help and it might get dangerous.'

'Vicky, as you were so fond of telling me before, we've still got no proof. Without definite proof, no one's going to take us seriously.'

'Then we can tell Mum and Dad,' I insisted.

'By the time they get back home from the antenatal

class, Beth and Sebastian will be on some Brazilian beach somewhere and that'll be that,' Gib said.

With a sigh, I gave up.

Half an hour later I'd had my shower at home and had changed my clothes and wolfed down a huge bowl of cornflakes. I was starving. We tried phoning Chaucy's mobile, but we just got the answering message. I was a bit freaked and gave Gib a worried look.

'He's fine. He's probably just on the Underground or something and can't get a signal.'

Then Gib and I had to run to school so we wouldn't be too late. All we could do now was wait for Chaucy.

Time crawled by on its stomach. Half an hour passed, then an hour – and still no Chaucy.

At breaktime Gib came up to me in the corridor. He looked about as worried as I felt – which didn't help. In fact, it made me feel worse.

'OK, face-ache! Where is he?' I asked Gib.

'I don't know,' Gib snapped back.

I glared at him. 'I knew it! I knew you should never have left Chaucy to it. Anything could've happened to him,' I ranted.

'He'll be all right,' Gib said doubtfully.

'What if Aunt Beth saw him? What if she met up with Sebastian and they both saw him? What if . . . ?'

'Hold on . . .' Gib protested.

'No, I won't hold on. We should never have involved him in the first place. What if . . . ?'

'Look! Nothing's happened to Chaucy,' Gib interrupted. 'He's probably still following her, I told him to stick to her like glue!'

'You . . . you don't think they might have switched to an earlier flight, do you?' I asked doubtfully.

Gib stared at me. 'Nah! They'd have left together then . . . wouldn't they?'

'Of course they would,' I decided firmly. 'We mustn't panic.'

'Vicky, don't do that to me!' Gib said, his hand on his chest over his heart. 'What I don't get is if they're not leaving until later, why'd they set off so early? Where d'you think Sebastian was going?'

I shrugged. 'I wish I knew,' I said unhappily.

Gib shook his head. 'I still can't believe it. Aunt Beth and Sebastian. They're supposed to be Dad's friends. Chaucy wouldn't do that to me! I mean, how could they? Especially now when Mum's pregnant.'

'Mum being pregnant has nothing to do with it,' I said. 'They saw a way of making a lot of money and they went for it, that's all. You know what grown-ups are like. A lot of them only care about money. Nothing else matters but having it and making it and getting more and more.'

'Well, they won't have it for long.' Gib's eyes narrowed. 'When Chaucy gets here, we'll go to the airport. We can work out a plan of action on the way there.'

'*If* Chaucy ever gets here,' I said.

My next lesson was double art. It might as well have been double Dutch for all the notice I took. When at last the buzzer went for the beginning of the lunch break, I was the first out of the art room. On my third circuit of the corridors, I spotted Chaucy and Gib deep in conversation. I headed straight for them.

'Where on earth have you been, Chaucy?' I said angrily. 'I was worried sick.'

Chaucy grinned at me. 'Were you?'

My face started to burn.

'It's not funny, you moron,' I said coldly. That wiped the smile off his face.

'There's no need to be like that,' he protested.

'Never mind her,' Gib interrupted. 'What happened? Where's Aunt Beth? Tell us everything.'

'I'll tell you all about it on the way to the airport,' Chaucy replied.

'Aunt Beth isn't already there, is she?' I asked, panicking again. 'It said sixteen-hundred hours on the tickets.'

'She stopped a taxi and asked to go somewhere. I didn't quite catch the name, but it wasn't Heathrow Airport,' Chaucy replied. 'Maybe she went to meet Sebastian somewhere first. We'd better get going though. They must be on their way to the airport by now.'

We all turned around and headed out of the school gates – making sure we weren't spotted by any of the teachers.

'So what happened, Chaucy?' I asked, as we walked down the road.

'Do you mind if I get a sandwich or something first? I'm starving,' Chaucy replied.

'Get on with it, Chaucy, before I strangle you!' Gib warned.

Chaucy was loving every moment in the spotlight.

'Well, I started following your aunt as directed . . .'

'She's not our aunt,' Gib interrupted.

'I'm only calling her what you two call her,' Chaucy said.

'Get on with it!' I begged.

'I followed *Beth* to the train station and I hopped into the same carriage as her. I made sure she didn't see me though. I sat in the set of seats behind her, but where I could see her when she got up.'

'Good move!' I approved.

Chaucy smiled at me, but this time I hardly minded.

'Anyway, we got off at Blackfriars about thirty minutes later. She walked through the station and I followed her. I should've got danger money for that bit. I was pushed and crushed and flattened by millions of rude grown-ups rushing to get to work. If *I* had to go to work each and every morning, I wouldn't be rushing,' Chaucy said scornfully. 'I didn't like that bit at all.'

'Chaucy . . .' Gib warned.

'All right! Keep your shirt on.' Chaucy frowned. 'Oh yes! Anyway, your aunt, I mean Beth, then went to another platform and hopped on a — what do they call it? — a City Thameslink train? We had to wait a while for that one so I had to hide out of the way. When the train finally did arrive, I almost got my head chopped off leaping on to it. A couple of stops later, Beth got off at Farringdon. I almost lost her then because a really snotty ticket collector looked closely at my travel pass and saw it didn't take me into the city. So he hit me with a penalty fare! Twenty quid! Lucky I had my emergency fund. When I finally got out of the station I was turning my head every which way trying to find her. Lucky she had on that huge white hat or I would have lost her for sure. But she was still well ahead of me. I had to run to catch her up. It was really exciting. I felt just like James Bond!'

'Where was she going?' I asked eagerly.

'I'm getting to that bit.'

Chaucy was being even more infuriating than usual. I had to breathe really deeply to control my temper.

'Now what was I saying? Oh yeah! Beth walked for a couple of minutes and stopped off at some bank along the way. She was only in there for a few minutes. When she came out again she carried on walking, before turning right into some street called Hatton something. Then she walked into a jeweller's shop.'

'A jeweller's?' I said, puzzled.

'Yep! The whole street was full of jewellery shops. Nothing but jewellery shops – and parking meters. I didn't pass one cake or sandwich shop! Oh yes, there was this big white building called The London Diamond Club just up from the jeweller's she went into.'

'What was she doing in there?' Gib asked.

'I couldn't exactly go in and ask, could I?' Chaucy said. 'I stood at the window and watched through the door. Beth spoke to some man behind the counter and handed him a piece of paper. He disappeared through a door at the back of the shop and came back a couple of minutes later, carrying a small blue box . . .'

'Did you see . . .'

'What was inside?'

Chaucy shook his head, regretfully. 'I was too far away.'

'How small was it? The size of a shoe box? The size of a matchbox?' I asked.

'About the size of my spider box,' Chaucy replied after a think.

'That doesn't help me much,' I pointed out. 'I haven't seen your spider box.'

I shivered at the thought of Chaucy keeping spiders in a box. No doubt he kept them in his bedroom. That was just the kind of nasty thing he would do, too.

'It's about that size.' Gib put his thumbs and his index fingers together to form a rectangle.

'Then what happened, Chaucy?'

'Well . . . Beth opened the box.' Chaucy shook his head with frustration. 'If I could just have got a bit closer . . .'

'You couldn't see anything at all?' I asked.

'Nothing,' Chaucy said sadly. 'Then Beth came out of the jeweller's with the box and hailed a taxi. Like I said, she asked to be taken somewhere but I didn't catch the name.'

'Hmm!' Gib said.

We looked at each other, deep in thought.

'Why would she go all the way into the city just to pick up some jewellery?' Gib asked. 'She could get jewellery anywhere around here.' We walked in silence as we tried to figure it out.

'Hatton Cross,' Chaucy said suddenly. 'That's the name of the street.'

As if the name of the street would help us!

We were almost at the tube station when I remembered where I'd seen the name Hatton Cross before.

'Chaucy, I thought you said you and Beth ended up in the city?' I asked with a frown.

'We did,' Chaucy replied. 'The street was just off Holborn Circus 'cause that's where we walked down to afterwards before Beth caught a taxi.'

'Don't you mean Hatton *Garden* – pillock!' I said.

199

'Hatton Garden is in the city. Hatton Cross is out by Heathrow.'

'That's it!' Chaucy pointed at me. 'Hatton Garden!'

I shook my head. Really!

The sunlit platform was practically deserted. I hated travelling by tube. All those dark tunnels and being so far underground. Thank goodness this station was out in the open. Somehow the sunlight made things seem a little less desperate. I'd had enough of being cooped up to last me a lifetime. I looked around again. There was no one immediately near us, but I still eyed the two other travellers on the platform with suspicion.

'Let's go over this again,' said Gib softly, even though we were alone. 'Beth and Sebastian got seven million pounds from Universal Bank . . .'

'Which is probably in that big suitcase you saw,' I said.

Gib nodded before he went on. 'And they're about to skip to Rio with it. Why did they put that million pounds into Dad's account? What was the point of it?'

'To stop Dad's checking program from being run,' I said.

'To get your dad out the way,' said Chaucy.

'To get everyone looking at Dad and away from them,' said Gib.

'Any or all of those reasons,' I said. 'If Beth knew she was going to write a program to nick some money then she'd have to test her program at some point and she'd have to plan when she was going to take out the money and how she was going to get at it and all sorts of other things. It's not the kind of thing you can do overnight.'

'What I don't get is why Universal Bank don't know about the seven million yet,' Gib said. 'They knew the next day that that one million had gone missing.'

'Are you sure they don't know?' Chaucy asked.

Gib nodded. 'Eric from the bank would've phoned Dad straightaway if the bank had lost more money. When we went home this morning, there was no message on the answering machine. Unless . . . unless Beth and Sebastian are taking the money out *today*.'

'Of course!' I breathed. 'That must be it. Maybe that large suitcase that Sebastian had was *empty*. Maybe he was going to pick up the money.'

'That makes sense.' Chaucy sounded surprised. 'If I was about to skip the country, I wouldn't take the money out until the last possible moment, in case something went wrong.'

'Besides which, they *couldn't* take it out any sooner,' I said. 'The bank would've been on to them. But if they got the money transferred immediately after this morning's batch job had finished, the bank wouldn't find out that something was wrong until after *tonight's* batch-job run.'

'So you really believe they're going to leave the

country with all that money?' asked Chaucy. 'I mean, that's an awful lot of money to carry.'

I had to admit, Chaucy had a point.

If only there was someone we could tell,' Gib said with a sudden burst of anger. 'They *mustn't* get away with it.'

'But we've still got no real proof – only the listing and the *ejones* name against the TIMETRV program in the batch library listing. By the time we get someone to listen to us and check it out, Beth and Sebastian's plane will be on its way *back* from Rio. Without proof – like the money they've stolen – no one will believe us. Not against two grown-ups. I mean, who's going to believe us if we say Beth, of all people, is running off with seven million of the bank's money?' I said glumly.

'Then let's work out what we should do next,' Gib said. 'And we'd better think fast. We haven't much time.'

'We've *got* to stop Sebastian and Beth from getting on their plane,' Chaucy said.

I sighed. Gib and Chaucy sighed with me.

'Chaucy . . . maybe you've done enough. You don't have to come with us. In fact, maybe you shouldn't get any more involved in case something goes wrong,' I said.

'But I'm already involved,' Chaucy said firmly. 'I want to help.'

I smiled at him. He was all right!

'OK, we know what time they're leaving and the airport,' Gib began. 'The next step must be to . . .'

'What terminal?' Chaucy butted in.

'Pardon?'

'What terminal are they flying from? Heathrow has got five,' Chaucy said.

I hadn't a clue and my horror-stricken face told him as much.

'I didn't see that bit on their tickets,' I whispered.

Gib glanced up at the train indicator board. 'Quick! We've still got four minutes before the train arrives. We'll phone the airport and find out.'

Gib fished his phone out of his pocket.

'Hurry up, Gib,' I urged.

'Phone directory enquiries to get the number,' Chaucy piped up.

'What should I ask for?' Gib asked doubtfully.

'Airport information?' I suggested. 'I know, just google it. Search for Heathrow Airport information.'

Gib did just that.

'Which airline?' Gib asked as he tapped at the screen on his phone.

'Er . . . Air France,' I whispered.

'Air France,' Gib repeated.

It took less than a minute to learn that Air France had four flights to Rio leaving that day. Apart from one at silly o'clock in the morning, they left at four o'clock, six o'clock and ten minutes past eight. Each flight stopped off in Paris, and each left from Terminal Four.

By this time our train had pulled into the station. We

raced onto the platform. Chaucy leaped onto the train just as the doors were closing. Using his body to keep the doors apart, he pushed at one of them, allowing Gib and me to duck under his arm to get on. Chaucy sprang towards us and the doors immediately smacked shut behind him.

'This is it,' Gib said quietly as the train began to move. 'If we mess this up, we're not going to get another chance.' Which didn't make any of us feel better.

'Don't worry, you two,' Chaucy said, trying to sound cheerful. 'We'll stop them, no bother.'

I looked from Chaucy to Gib and back again. They both looked worried.

Do I look like them? I wondered. I must do.

'We'll do all right,' Gib said firmly.

I wished I could be sure.

Chapter Fourteen

Holiday Dressing

We sat in silence for the last two tube stops before Heathrow, Terminal 4. My stomach was rocking inside me. The tube was stuffy and smelly and now jam-packed full of people. I would never have guessed that there'd be so many wanting to go to Heathrow in the afternoon, but in our carriage it was standing room only.

I couldn't wait to get off. Yet I knew that once we got out it would be all up to us. And that thought was so scary. If the plan Chaucy, Gib and I had come up with didn't work then all the work we'd done so far would be for nothing. Sebastian and Beth would get away scot free. And worst of all, by far, Dad might end up in prison.

So this was it.

Now I wished we'd told someone, tried to get some help. But who would believe us? Adults tended to stick together over things they considered important – like money. And the lies we'd told to get this far! By the time Mum and Dad knew the whole truth we'd have stopped Sebastian and Beth taking all that money out of the country. We'd have proved that Dad was innocent. So the theory was that our parents wouldn't be too angry.

I looked at Gib and he looked at me. Neither of us said a word. Gib's lips were set in a frown. He looked like he never wanted to smile again. I glanced down at my watch for the umpteenth time in about thirty seconds.

'Vicky, we're here.' Chaucy nudged my arm as at last we reached the stop for Heathrow, Terminal 4.

We travelled along the long, grey corridor with painted abstracts on each wall, then up in one of the lifts to the departure level – all in total silence. If I thought the tube was bad then the airport terminal was far, far worse. I'd never seen so many people milling about. The whole place was huge. There were queues and check-in counters and noise everywhere. And as I gawped, two policemen strolled by carrying guns! It was so strange to see armed police just wandering around, mingling with the tourists..

I'd been to the airport before but I'd been a lot younger then and I could hardly remember anything about it. And, of course, that had been with Mum and Dad. My heart was jumping about all over my body now. I was terrified. I felt minuscule amongst all these people and all this bustle and jumble and noise. I looked at Gib and Chaucy. Thankfully, they both looked how I felt – nervous, to say the least.

'Where's the information about when the planes leave?' Gib asked.

I pointed. A number of TV monitors were suspended from the ceiling with departure information on them. All three of us walked over to the closest monitor and stared up at it. The Rio flight wasn't on it.

'That's a fat lot of good,' Gib said with disgust.

We walked around, waiting for more flight information to be displayed and wondering if our plan stood any chance at all of working.

In the centre of the hall, we noticed more monitors.

'Rio . . . Rio . . .' Gib muttered as we each scanned down them.

'It isn't there!' Chaucy said dejectedly. 'The only Air France flight I can see is going to Paris.'

I looked up at the monitor, and suddenly something clicked in my brain. Something from when I was looking at the airline tickets. Flight AF2581 . . . at 1600 . . . to Paris. That must be it!

I tore over to the Air France desk and practically launched myself at the smiling, blonde woman in a smart uniform.

'Excuse me,' I said, 'Your flight to Rio – do you have to get on a flight to Paris first?'

'Yes, that's right,' she replied. 'We don't fly direct from London to Rio. First you have to fly to Charles de Gaulle Airport in Paris, and then change planes. The next flight is AF2581 – I can check you and your parents in here if you like?'

'No, that's OK, thanks. I was just checking!'

I legged it back to Gib and Chaucy.

'That's it!' I pointed at the monitor. 'AF2581 to Paris, taking off at sixteen-hundred hours. That's the first leg of the trip to Rio!'

Almost directly opposite the monitors was a sign which said:

PASSPORT HOLDERS ONLY BEYOND THIS POINT

'Do you think they've already gone through?' Gib said what I was reluctantly thinking.

'Of course not,' I said firmly, crossing my fingers. 'Why should they go through this early? It's not one o'clock yet.'

'But we don't know for sure that they haven't,' Gib said.

'Victoria is right. They wouldn't go through this early,' Chaucy replied. 'Chill out, Gib! We'll get them.'

I smiled at Chaucy's confidence, hoping it was infectious.

'Right. I'll go and do my bit now. Don't get lost, you two,' I said.

'Don't worry – we won't,' Gib said, his voice sharp with nerves. 'Just make sure you keep your eyes open.'

I walked away from them back towards the Air France desk.

'They couldn't have gone through yet,' I told myself. *Please don't let them get away with it. Please don't.* I muttered the words over and over again like a song or a spell.

The sign over the counter said 'Business Class'. This time I had to stand behind two people, impatiently waiting my turn. At last, they moved on after being served, and the check-in woman smiled across at me from over the counter.

'Er, excuse me,' I began. 'Me again! Can you help? Could you tell me if Beth and Sebastian Carter have checked in yet for the four o'clock flight to Paris?'

Her smile faded. 'I'm sorry. We're not allowed to give out that information.'

'But it's really important,' I pleaded.

The woman shrugged. 'I'm sorry.'

I wanted to scream. I was falling down at the first hurdle.

'Thanks anyway,' I mumbled, walking away from her.

Someone was waving at me. It was Chaucy, with Gib next to him. They were standing by the escalators. I ran over to them.

'It's no good,' I puffed. 'The woman at the desk wouldn't tell me whether they'd checked in or not.'

'I'll find out,' Chaucy said, his face determined. Before we could stop him or ask any questions, off he strode.

'Where's he going?' I asked Gib.

'Haven't a clue.'

'Shouldn't we go with him?'

'If he'd wanted us with him, he would have said so,' Gib said calmly.

Five minutes later we found out where Chaucy had gone.

'Would Mrs Beth Carter and her husband, Mr Sebastian Carter, please report to the information desk,' a man's voice boomed out over the loudspeaker system.

Gib and I looked at each other.

'Chaucy!' we exclaimed.

'Where's the information desk?' I asked.

'I'll find it. You wait here and watch the check-in desks in case Beth and Sebastian turn up,' Gib ordered.

A few minutes later the same message came out again over the loudspeakers.

I finally caught sight of the information desk but I couldn't see Gib or Chaucy, and I couldn't see any sign of Beth and Sebastian. All this looking around was giving me a crick in my neck. I scanned the check-in desks. Still nothing. I kept looking around, desperate to catch sight of our quarry.

'Anything?' Chaucy asked, appearing before me from out of nowhere with Gib close behind him.

I shook my head. 'Not a sausage. I take it they didn't turn up at the information desk?'

Chaucy and Gib shook their heads.

'They can't be here yet,' Gib said hopefully.

'Right then. Time for phase two. Let's split up again,' I said. 'When they do arrive they'll have to check in first, so between us we should spot them. Remember, the first one to see them has to go into action and the others stand by to act as back-up. Keep your eyes on the Air France desks. Don't forget what you have to do. I'll be over there where I can keep an eye on the passengers going through Security.'

We split up again, each of us going in a different direction.

The minutes ticked by too slowly. Standing still while everyone else rushed around me was really strange. Like watching the world go by all speeded up without being a part of it. I'd felt like that a lot recently. Even looking at my real mum and dad's photo over the last couple of days didn't help any more. In fact, it made me feel more sad. Like I was stuck out on the middle of an island somewhere and no one knew I was there. And no one cared that I was there. I knew I was feeling sorry for myself, but it didn't change the way I felt. I told myself I had more than a lot of people. I had someone to call Mum and Dad, even if they weren't my real parents. So why did I feel that it wasn't enough? I never used to feel like that . . . not really. Not all the time. Not until Gib and I had our big quarrel. I wanted to know more about my real parents, so much more, and there was no one to tell me. I wanted to find out who they were, what they liked and didn't like – as

211

if in finding out about them, I would find out about myself.

Leaning against the wall next to a cash machine, I had nothing to do but think – and my thoughts were making me feel pretty miserable. It felt like even my adopted parents were slipping away from me. Dad was in trouble. Mum was having another baby. And Gib? Gib thought of me as an intruder, as someone who didn't belong. And he was right. I didn't belong. Not really.

I stood and brooded while the minutes ticked away. I wasn't sure what I wanted any more. I only knew that this – whatever *this* was – wasn't it. I didn't want to stay where I wasn't wanted. *I wouldn't* stay where I wasn't wanted. But hadn't Dad said that he and Mum thought of me as their real daughter? And I believed him. So maybe the problem was Gib. Or maybe the problem was just me . . .

'Stop them. Stop those two! They've stolen some money. They've stolen seven million pounds!'

Gib's voice instantly stopped my daydreaming. I straightened up, looking in the direction of his voice. I saw Gib run up to Beth and Sebastian who were standing in the queue for passengers travelling first-class. I couldn't see Beth properly – she was partially hidden behind Sebastian and her face was obscured by a white hat with a huge brim. But I could see Sebastian all right. He was carrying the two suitcases – one large and one small – that Gib had told me about before. He was dressed in a cream-coloured shirt and trousers and wore mirrored sunglasses.

Sebastian and Beth turned to each other, before glaring at Gib. I dashed over to them, stumbling in my haste to get there. I wasn't going to leave Gib alone with them.

'Help me, someone!' Gib shouted at the top of his lungs.

Apart from me, no one was moving. It was as if everyone around had suddenly sprouted roots. They stared at Gib with astonished faces but nobody budged. Sebastian took off his glasses to glare at Gib, more to intimidate him than for any other reason, I reckoned.

'Help me, someone – please!' Gib shouted desperately. 'They've stolen money from my dad's bank!'

'Why you . . .' Sebastian's expression turned from furious to murderous as he leaped towards Gib, making a grab for him.

Gib lashed out to knock Sebastian's arm away. Sebastian was faster though. With fingers of iron he grabbed Gib by the arms.

'What do you think you're playing at?' Sebastian asked, absolutely livid.

I launched myself up into the air and leaped on his back.

'Let him go, you creep!' I shouted.

Sebastian swung around in surprise. He tried to prise my arms from around his neck with one hand while he kept Gib in his clutches with the other. I was determined to get him to release Gib, but deep inside the thought sprang up that Sebastian couldn't have done better if we'd paid him. The moment the crowd saw him going for Gib, they sprang into action.

'Sebastian, don't be a fool!' Beth called out, but the warning came too late.

Everyone started to move in then. Two men from the next check-in queue ran over and angrily pulled Sebastian's hands off Gib, while a woman behind him in the queue screamed for the police while beating Sebastian over the head with her handbag. I dropped down on to the ground before she ended up hitting me as well.

'That boy is lying!' Beth shouted at the crowd which was gathering around now.

'I'm not!' Gib protested. 'They've stolen seven million from my dad's bank and blamed it on my dad. Look in their suitcases. They've stolen the money, I swear.'

'What's he talking about . . . ?'

'Is someone making a film . . . ?'

'Does that man know this boy then . . . ?'

I could have stomped up and down with frustration. Wasn't *anyone* going to do something?

'What's going on here then?' asked a tall man wearing a charcoal-grey jacket.

'Who are you?' asked one of the men who was still holding onto Sebastian.

'Detective Sergeant Andrews, Heathrow Police Division,' the man answered.

'This boy says these two have stolen some money,' said the other man, who now relinquished his hold on Sebastian.

'They stole the money from my dad's bank. They're rotten, stinking thieves,' Gib said earnestly. 'And now they're trying to run off to Rio with all that money.'

'Is that likely?' Beth said smoothly. 'This child is obviously just playing a joke. A joke that's in very poor taste.'

'I'm *not*,' Gib said indignantly.

Sergeant Andrews looked from Beth to Gib and frowned deeply. I had to admit, Beth looked very believable. Not the sort of woman to steal, not the sort of woman who looked like she *had* to steal.

She looked totally different. Her hair wasn't in its usual ponytail, it was loose. She had on a wide-brimmed, floppy white hat with a black band around it and wore a white jacket with black lapels and a white skirt. She even wore black and white shoes that matched the rest of her outfit.

I'd always thought she wasn't particularly interested in clothes or how she looked. I'd never seen her looking so smart. She'd even changed her earrings. Instead of the usual gold studs, she wore long, dangly earrings, shaped like pears. Each of the pears was at least two and a half centimetres long. They had to be clip-ons.

215

Anything else would have pulled her earlobes off.

'Really! This is too ridiculous.' Beth smiled, a frosty, angry smile.

'We don't even know this boy,' Sebastian said to the policeman.

'I mean, do we look like criminals, officer?' Beth laughed.

'Criminals don't walk around with that word stamped on their foreheads, madam,' Sergeant Andrews replied politely.

'Aren't you going to arrest them or something?' Gib asked. 'Beth took seven million pounds from Dad's bank. She and Dad both work at Universal Bank.'

'This is too much.' Beth wasn't laughing any more. She had a face like thunder. 'If you don't mind, officer, my husband and I have a plane to catch.'

'Just what is your name, madam?' Sergeant Andrews asked.

'Beth. Beth Carter,' Beth replied.

'Her full name is Elizabeth Janine Carter,' I said quickly. 'Ask her if you don't believe me.'

'And who are you?' The sergeant frowned at me.

I looked at Gib. He was watching me.

'I know him,' I said, pointing to Gib. 'We're friends – sort of.'

Gib opened his mouth to speak.

'I'm with him,' I interrupted firmly. 'That's all.'

'Hmm!' The sergeant turned back to Beth.

'Is your full name Elizabeth Janine Carter or not?'

Beth didn't answer.

'May I see your passport please?' Sergeant Andrews asked.

'Yes, that is my full name,' admitted Beth reluctantly.

By this time a considerable crowd had gathered around, listening to every word.

'Is that right?' the sergeant asked slowly.

'Look, we can explain . . .' Sebastian began. 'You don't want to believe a word either of them says, especially Victoria. And Gib's just as bad. We only . . .'

'So you do know these children?' Sergeant Andrews interjected.

Sebastian's face fell. Mine lit up.

'I thought you just said that you didn't know this boy?' the sergeant said suspiciously.

'I . . . that is, we don't know them . . . very well,' Sebastian said feebly.

'Is Gib your name?' the policeman asked.

Gib nodded. 'It's my nickname. My real name is Richard Gibson, but everyone calls me Gib.'

'You don't know these children very well,' Sergeant Andrews began, 'but you do know them well enough to know this boy's nickname.'

'I can explain . . .' Sebastian said quickly.

'I'm sure you can. And I'd like to hear this explanation. I think we'd all better go to a private room where I can find out exactly what's going on here.'

Chapter Fifteen

The Truth

'If you'll all come with me,' said Sergeant Andrews, 'there's a room we can use on the next floor down.'

The policeman walked alongside Sebastian and Beth, while Gib and I walked behind them. The crowd parted like the Red Sea to let us through. I wanted to speak to Gib but I didn't dare open my mouth. For starters, where was Chaucy? We went down the escalator and headed for a blue door to our left. The room inside had in it a large wooden table and a blue carpet. There were a number of chairs against the wall and in front of the table. There were no windows but the light overhead was very bright. Sergeant Andrews waited until we were all in the room before shutting the door. Then he sat down at the table.

'Right then. Let's start with you,' the sergeant said to me. 'What's your name?'

'Victoria.'

'Victoria what?'

'Just Victoria,' I replied.

I could feel Gib looking at me but I didn't look back at him.

'Hmm!' the sergeant said. 'All right. Just Victoria will do for now. Gib, you start.'

Gib took a deep breath. I looked at him and smiled.

'Beth works at Universal Bank. That's where our dad works . . . as the Internal Auditing Manager. Beth's a programmer. That's how she fixed it so that she could take seven million pounds from the bank for herself. Now she and Sebastian are escaping to Rio with all that money.'

I grinned at Gib. I couldn't have done better myself. He didn't see me though. He was nervously watching Sergeant Andrews.

'Sergeant Andrews, feel free to check my handbag and our luggage. Sebastian and I have about five thousand pounds on us and that's it.' Beth smiled. 'I changed half the money into American dollars and the rest into traveller's cheques. And what's more, Sebastian has the bank receipt to prove it.'

I licked my lips. Something was wrong. Beth looked far too smug, too relaxed.

'First things first. Is Gib right? Do you work at Universal Bank as a programmer?' the sergeant asked.

Beth looked at Gib and me, her face a mask.

'Yes, it is true, but I can explain . . .' she began.

'Five thousand pounds is a lot of money to be carrying on you – no matter what currency it's in,' said Sergeant Andrews.

'It's all the money we have in the world,' Sebastian explained. 'We decided to make this the holiday of a lifetime – the best hotels, the best food . . . We're having a second honeymoon. That money represents every penny we have in the world. And as Beth said, we do have proof that the cash is ours. Just a minute, I'll show you.'

'A receipt doesn't mean anything,' Gib dismissed quickly. 'Beth works at Universal Bank. She could have forged that receipt.'

'Really! I think you've been watching too much television,' Beth scoffed. 'Sergeant, please feel free to call my bank. They'll tell you that it was a perfectly legitimate transaction.'

'There you are,' Sebastian said, after searching through his wallet. He handed a slip of paper over to Sergeant Andrews who scrutinized it before handing it back.

'That seems to be in order,' Sergeant Andrews said.

'Sergeant Andrews, they've got a lot more than five thousand on them,' I said. 'They've got seven million. Sebastian told me so.'

'Oh, he did, did he?' the sergeant said, in a tone that told me I shouldn't have told him that.

'It was just a joke, officer,' Sebastian laughed. 'You know what fertile imaginations children have. I was just humouring her.'

'Where is this five thousand? May I see it?' Sergeant Andrews asked.

Beth shrugged. 'Help yourself. It's in the small suit-case.'

Gib and I moved to stand beside the sergeant as he opened the case. The front of the suitcase was filled with pile upon pile of green money. Dollars. I'd never seen American dollars before. Behind the money, the top two rows were blue and red traveller's cheques. It all represented more money than I'd ever seen in my life. Sergeant Andrews counted the money with quick, expert fingers.

'That seems about right,' he said at last.

'I told you.' Beth smiled at Gib and me. 'Five thousand. Not a penny more or less.'

'Look in the large suitcase. The seven million must be in there,' Gib said.

'I don't think so, Gib.' The sergeant smiled. 'You'd need a lot more than one suitcase for seven million pounds, no matter how you packed it.'

'They *have* got seven million on them. Honest they have,' I said. 'Aren't you even going to look?'

'Oh, this is ridiculous.' Beth knelt down by her larger suitcase and within moments had opened it. She threw back the top. We leaned forward expectantly.

It was full of clothes.

'Seb and I decided to share one suitcase as we intend to buy most of our clothes when we get out there.' Beth picked up a few items to show the lining at the bottom of the suitcase. 'See! There's no money in here. I've nothing up my sleeves either.'

Where was all that money? Gib and I looked at each other, horror-stricken.

'Shall I tell you what this is really all about, officer?' Sebastian said, glaring at me. 'Their father was caught trying to take one million pounds from Universal Bank. He's been in front of a magistrate and he's now waiting for a date for his trial. So these two decided to try and pin the crime on someone else. They reckon they can get their father off the hook by putting my wife and me on it.'

'That's a dirty lie!' Gib exploded.

The sergeant looked from me to Gib.

'So you two are brother and sister?' he asked.

'No. I'm adopted,' I told him.

It was the first time I'd ever said the words without being prompted first. And, surprisingly, I didn't mind. I didn't mind at all. I didn't even mind his expression – an expression I'd seen many, many times before. A mixture of interest and pity.

That's what he feels, I thought. It doesn't have to be how I feel.

I was Victoria Murchie who'd been adopted and had her name changed to Victoria Gibson. But most importantly, I was Victoria. No one could change that or take that away from me.

'So can we go now, officer?' Beth asked, shutting the case again.

'Of course, Mrs Carter. I'm sorry you were inconvenienced,' said the policeman.

'You're not going to let them go, are you?' Gib exclaimed.

'You can't,' I pleaded.

'The game is over, Gib and Vicky. You've had your little joke. As you can see, we don't have that kind of money,' Beth laughed. 'I wish we did.'

Beth straightened up from her suitcase. Sebastian picked it up.

'Don't let them go,' I begged. 'The money must be somewhere.'

'Where? In our pockets? Or maybe it's in our shoes?' Sebastian laughed.

And he was laughing at us. Beth and Sebastian made for the door. Then my brain clicked in. Hatton Garden. Loads and loads of jewellers' shops . . .

'It's not cash . . . it's jewellery. Beth went to Hatton Garden this morning!' I shouted. 'That's how they're doing it. Jewellery.'

'If there's nothing else . . .' Beth said with disdain. She and Sebastian headed for the door, sharpish. I turned to Sergeant Andrews.

'Stop them!' I said desperately. 'They must have some jewellery in the suitcase worth seven million. Please . . .'

'That's right. Beth did go to Hatton Garden this morning.' Gib backed me up.

223

'Is that right, Mrs Carter? Did you go to Hatton Garden?' Sergeant Andrews asked.

'No, I did not,' Beth replied haughtily.

'Yes she did,' I contradicted angrily. 'After they locked me in their cellar all night and left me there. If it wasn't for Gib, I'd still be in their house.'

'Locked you in their . . . ?' the sergeant began.

'She lives in a fantasy world,' Beth said dismissively with a wave of her hand. 'Even her own mother will tell you that.'

'Liar!' Gib shouted at her. 'Mum would never say anything like that about Victoria. Please, Sergeant Andrews, you've got to look in their suitcases. It's jewels. I know it is.'

The policeman looked at Gib and me. Our eyes, our faces, our whole bodies pleaded with him.

'Would you mind?' The sergeant smiled apologetically at Sebastian and Beth. 'It would clear this up once and for all.'

Beth and Sebastian exchanged a look.

'Very well then,' Beth said with impatience. 'But that's it. We have a plane to catch and I've had just about enough of this nonsense.'

As Sergeant Andrews squatted down to open the large suitcase, Beth and Sebastian turned to smile at us. And then I knew that the jewels couldn't be in the suitcase. No way would they be so calm about their suitcase being searched if there was any possibility of jewels being found in there. I looked at Sebastian. He put on his sunglasses again, still smirking at us. I turned to Beth. She looked like the cat who'd got the cream. She slowly shook her head at me, still looking smug. I had to squinch up my eyes. Her large pear-drop earrings glinted in the artificial light of the room and dazzled me. Sergeant Andrews closed the suitcase.

'I've had enough of this,' Sebastian fumed. 'If there's nothing else, Sergeant, we have a plane to catch.'

'Of course, sir. I'll escort you to your check-in desk.'

I turned to Gib, stricken. We'd failed. Dad . . .

Sebastian and Beth headed out the door and up the escalator to the departure lounge. The sergeant stood next to Gib and me, behind them. I felt totally numb. I couldn't feel a thing. We'd failed . . .

At the top of the escalator, Sebastian and Beth turned. They were still smirking. And Beth's dangly earrings were swinging, swinging.

Then I realized. I ran forward and stretched up to pull off Beth's right earring. Beth screamed. Sebastian lurched at me. I ducked. I ran for the sergeant as Sebastian made another grab for me.

'It's the earrings! It's the earrings!' I yelled. 'They must be real or something.'

I held out my hand towards Sergeant Andrews. Frowning deeply, he took the earring out of my hand.

'Now, young lady, you can't . . .'

'Look out!' Gib shouted. 'Sebastian's making a run for it.'

'Sebastian . . .' Beth called after him.

All I could see was Sebastian's rapidly retreating back. The sergeant sprang after him. We were right behind the sergeant. Then we saw someone dive at Sebastian's legs, rugby tackling him to the ground. It was Chaucy.

'Get him, Chaucy!' I yelled.

Beth took a quick look around, her eyes wild before she tried to make a break for it herself.

'Oh no you don't!' The sergeant grabbed her by the arm. 'You stay right there.'

Sergeant Andrews talked into his walkie-talkie as he ran to help Chaucy.

'Quick, Gib,' I said, dragging him after me. We moved to stand in front of Beth.

'If you want to go anywhere, you're going to have to get by Gib and me first,' I hissed at her.

Moments later, four police officers – three men and one woman – arrived from out of nowhere. One policeman and the woman ran straight for a now raging Sebastian. The other two policemen came up to us and took Beth by the arms.

They started to walk away. Gib suddenly darted forward and pulled the other earring off Beth's ear. Beth tried to stop him but the policemen had a firm hold on her.

'You . . .' Beth snarled at Gib and me. 'I'll get you two for this. You see if I don't.'

'You won't be getting anyone or anything,' Sergeant Andrews interrupted. 'You're coming with us.'

'Gotcha!' Gib mocked.

'Pass over those earrings before anything else happens to them,' said Sergeant Andrews.

Gib handed over his one. I held my earring up to look at it. It was beautiful. It looked just like polished glass. I handed it over.

'Constable, could you bring the suitcases,' Sergeant Andrews said to one of the policemen who had Beth by the arm. 'I want to go through them again with a fine-toothed comb.'

Gib and I grinned at each other – relief and happiness all mixed up. I couldn't believe it. We'd done it! Beth and Sebastian had been caught. I was actually trembling and my heart was dancing inside me. We'd stopped them. *We'd done it!* It was over.

'I want you two to come with me,' Sergeant Andrews said over his shoulder. 'You both have a lot of explaining to do.'

We were sitting in a room in the police station, each of us sipping at a carton of apple juice we'd been given. Dad was coming to pick us up and Chaucy's parents had been notified and they were coming for him. According to Sergeant Andrews, none of our parents were exactly thrilled with us.

'I'll explain what's happened to them,' Sergeant

Andrews said and winked at us. 'Just as you explained it to us. I think once your parents know what you've done, they'll be very proud of you.'

Gib and I looked at each other glumly. It was past six o'clock. Mum and Dad were each going to make sticky splats on the ceiling at this one. Six o'clock. And we had ducked out of half a day of school! Sergeant Andrews left the room.

'I won't be seeing any more pocket money for the rest of the year,' Chaucy sighed. 'The rest of the year? I mean the rest of my life!'

Now it was all over I felt strange. Like a balloon with all the air let out. What would happen to me now that Dad was going to be all right?

Sergeant Andrews came back into the room, followed by a woman with greying hair cut short and wearing glasses with bright green frames. She had on a matching bright green suit that looked really weird.

'Gib, Vicky, Chaucy, this is Detective Macon, our jewellery expert,' Sergeant Andrews told us.

'So you're the children who are responsible for bringing those wonderful diamond earrings to my attention.' Detective Macon smiled, revealing a mouth filled to overflowing with huge teeth. 'You should be very proud of yourselves. Each of those earrings is a twenty-two-carat diamond. And they're flawless! Exceptional! The cut, the clarity – I haven't seen anything like them in a long, long time.'

The cut? The clarity? I hadn't a clue what she was talking about and, glancing at Gib and Chaucy, I saw they were equally bemused.

Detective Macon's smile broadened – which I would have thought was impossible.

'There are four criteria for deciding what makes a fine gemstone,' she beamed. 'The carat value, which is just another way of saying the weight, the cut, the clarity and the colour. It's known as the four Cs. And I have to tell you that Mrs Carter's earrings were superior in all four categories. Easily worth the three and a half million she paid for each one of them. And, of course, they would have got more for them in Brazil.'

I'd held three and a half million pounds in my hand! Wow!

'I thought they were just bits of glass. They looked a bit big and tacky,' I said. 'Not Aunt Beth's usual style at all. That's what made me realize that they must be proper jewels. That and the fact that she was in Hatton Garden this morning.'

'Three and a half million dangling from each ear.' Chaucy whistled.

'Very daring. A very daring plan.' Detective Macon nodded.

'What about the money?' Gib asked. 'Did she transfer that to her own bank account or Sebastian's?'

'Yeah, I'd like to know that bit,' I piped up.

'Mrs Carter has admitted that the money went

229

straight into an account she set up at another bank,' said Sergeant Andrews. 'She transferred the money from Universal Bank to her new bank account and then all she had to do was get a banker's cheque for the money this morning. All that was left after that was to pick up the diamonds.'

'So I was right. Universal wouldn't know the money had gone until after tonight's batch run,' I said.

'Well, I wouldn't know about that bit,' smiled Sergeant Andrews, 'but well done, all of you! Now, Detective Macon and I are just going to sort out a few things so we'll leave you alone for a couple of minutes. Will you be all right?'

'Fine,' we all said.

I bent my head as they left the room. I was so tired.

'Chaucy, go to the loo or something,' Gib commanded.

'But I don't need to . . .' I sensed rather than saw Chaucy look from Gib to me and back again. 'Oh, I see . . . OK.' He stood up and left the room.

'At the airport, why did you tell Sergeant Andrews that you were only my friend?' Gib asked quietly.

'I know I shouldn't have even said that,' I replied fiercely. 'I did change it. I said you were just someone I knew. So don't start.'

'But why would you want to say something like that?' Gib asked.

'That's what you want me to say, isn't it?' I replied.

The football was back in my throat, choking, and my eyes were stinging the life out of me. 'Your dad is going to be all right now and your mum can stop worrying about him. You must be pleased.'

'They're your mum and dad too,' Gib said.

I glared at him. 'No they aren't. My mum and dad are dead. They drowned to get away from me – remember?'

Gib looked down at his hands on the table. 'I'm sorry I said that. I didn't mean it. I just wanted . . . I'm sorry.'

I stared at him. He'd never said sorry to me in his life.

'It doesn't matter,' I lied with a shrug.

'Yes, it does. I've tried to say sorry lots of times. Saturday in the garden . . . I even changed into the T-shirt you bought me to show you I was sorry . . . This morning . . . I was sorry the moment I'd said all that rubbish. I didn't mean it, Victoria.'

'It doesn't matter.' I shrugged again. 'Anyway, you and Chaucy can go home but I'm not coming with you. I'm going to stay here. Or maybe go to a foster home.'

'Why would you want to do a stupid thing like that?' Gib scowled.

'It's not stupid. I won't stay where I'm not wanted. You should be overjoyed. It's what you wanted, isn't it?'

'Of course not,' Gib said, looking straight at me. 'What would I do without my big sister.'

The room went very quiet after he said that. I couldn't move, couldn't blink, couldn't breathe. And

I couldn't believe it! Gib had never, *ever* called me his sister – big or otherwise.

Gib grimaced at me, the tips of his ears red, his expression embarrassed. That did it! The snot-rag made me do something I swore I'd never do again in front of him. I burst into tears.

'Oh, come on,' Gib said, even more embarrassed now. 'Don't cry. We're going home soon. And we proved our dad didn't take that money.'

I wiped my face but I couldn't stop crying. I nodded.

'I guess so,' I sniffed.

'Besides, who would Chaucy witter on about all the time if you didn't come home?' Gib smiled.

That's my brother. Sometimes he can be a right snot-rag and a half!

About the author

MALORIE BLACKMAN is acknowledged as one of today's most imaginative and convincing writers for young readers. *Noughts & Crosses* has won several prizes, including the Children's Book Award. Malorie is also the only author to have won the Young Telegraph/Gimme 5 Award twice with *Hacker* and *Thief!* Her work has appeared on screen, with *Pig-Heart Boy*, which was shortlisted for the Carnegie Medal, being adapted into a BAFTA-award-winning TV serial. Malorie has also written a number of titles for younger readers.

In 2005, Malorie was honoured with the Eleanor Farjeon Award in recognition of her distinguished contribution to the world of children's books.

In 2008, she received an OBE for her services to children's literature.

www.**malorieblackman**.co.uk